# Ravena

## The Eight Book Two

### Sharilyn Skye

Copyright 2019 by Sharilyn Skye
All Rights Reserved
Paperback ISBN 978133313438
First Edition: November 2019
Revision February 2021
Cover Design: PaigeLCroPhotography/ Dark Horse Publishing
Cover Photo: Milla Fedotora/ Dreamstime

Dark Horse Publishing

Morgantown, WV

I have my ship,

And all my flags are a flying'.

~**Crosby, Stills, Nash**

"The world breaks everyone, and afterward, some are strong at the broken places."~**Ernest Hemingway**

"Out of suffering have emerged the strongest souls; the most massive characters are seared with scars."~ **Khalil Gibran**

# Chapter One

## Ravena

My life began, in truth, the day Ari helped me kill Rowan. How he received the gift of one of The Eight, I will never know. After his death, Lochlann told me that the Queen had initially tried to convince the brothers to take Ari, her own daughter. Only Rowan was vain to his core. He believed that the only proper coloring for a true Fae was black hair and blue eyes. Like the four brothers, I was forced to accept as mates-like me.

My name is Ravena, and I am the second youngest of the last eight females born to this Goddess-forsaken land. I had three brothers who were murdered before I was born. The land does not need more males, so says the Queen, but she's nice enough to allow them to be mothered for a short time before she kills them. This is her only concession to their parents. My mother was broken before I was ever taken from her to be raised like livestock by someone else.

Talamh na Sithe is dying. It's dead already, if you ask me, which no one did. Aramea's plan to save the land involves breeding the last eight females to the strongest or most beautiful men in hopes of producing children.

She thinks that since these matings have been examined and studied by her genetic doctors that they will be successful, but the Fae have been fucking in Faerie for decades, and no children have been born since Ari. Not even boys. Shame on all the Daoine Sidhe.

We're being punished for crimes we did not commit, but that's beside the point. I was taken from my family, from my seven sisters, and brought to the little house next to Ari's bakery. I couldn't breathe fresh air until the eldest brother's poisoned body was taken and burned.

After weeks of forcible sex, which wasn't quite rape since I knew I would be having sex with these men and accepted it from the beginning. Still, it wasn't not rape either, as he liked for me to fight him and only climaxed when he made me cry. His brand of torture did not stop until I pleased him with my tears.

And the Queen had begged him to take her daughter because she knew. Of that, I am sure. There is no love lost between Aramea and Airmed.

I hate crying. I am so not a crier. We had classes on everything from sex to archery to the beatings men sometimes give, but we never had a class in crying. In fact, we were taught not to cry. It was annoying to have to learn, but learn I did. Let me tell you.

So when Ari told me to feed that calloused son of a bitch poison and take him to bed for his pleasure, friend, let me tell you I wailed, shrieked, and carried on until he had the biggest orgasm of his life, thus sending his heart into a standstill, thank the Goddess. And thank you, Ari.

Lochlann was with us, as Rowan demanded, and Ari suggested. He saw the whole thing and assuredly felt nothing but glee over his brother's death. If they gave awards for theatrical performances, I would have received the highest one, but everyone in this house would have been contenders.

Rowan was not a nice man.

His brothers had endured his sick attention for decades. As females are in short supply in Talamh na Sithe, men tend to be together out of need, if not desire. It's commonplace but not among brothers. Among siblings, it is plain wrong. The three remaining Rowan brothers had suffered horribly, sexually and otherwise. No one cried a tear beside his funeral pyre. However, we kept our eyes lowered so the Queen wouldn't notice.

We went home afterward and stripped off our mourning clothes and danced like crazed animals under the light of the moon. They did not try to touch me. Not once.

I had my own room for the first time in my life. Rory gave me his and took Rowan's, knowing I could never sleep in that horrible place again. I redecorated, and they bought me everything I could want to be comfortable and then some.

We healed.

The remaining brothers were kind, despite their difficult start in life. They were of the last generation of males allowed to live and were not as old as the other girls' mates. They had never been unkind. Not exactly. Had they stood up to Rowan when he beat me? They had not. Nor did they stand up to him when he forced his sexual deviance on all of us, but then they were victims too, and I blame them not even a little for what happened under this roof.

A lifetime of abuse can cause two outcomes. One being that the abused learns to delight in doling out pain, the other being that the abused stays kind in their soul and abhors any and all types of mistreatment. Finn, Lochlann, and Rory walked the last path. There is not a mean bone in their bodies.

They took this to the extreme of not touching me for days, not even gently. We avoided one another and lived in companionable silence until I began spending more time with Ari, then they watched like raptors. Learning all they could.

It was sad, actually. My mates had no idea what social norms looked like or how one should behave around women in polite company. They watched Lann, Saige, Seal, and Laith with unabashed zeal, trying to learn what put such big smiles on Ari's face and caused her laughter to echo through the streets of the capital.

I walked from Ari's bakery through our home's door one evening to find our entire house redone and dinner on the table. I knew they were trying to move forward. After days of stasis and fear of being free, we could finally breathe. It was like Rowan's death wasn't real until that moment.

I went to them one by one, placing chaste kisses on their lips. I wasn't afraid of them, not now. Rowan's evil went up in the flames of his funeral pyre and did not reside in these men trying so hard to learn to live someplace other than his shadow.

Dinner was excellent.

We stuffed ourselves on meat, bread, and pastries from Ari's bakery. After we went outside to enjoy the last rays of the spring sun in Talamh na Sithe, and for the first time, I thought maybe I was wrong and that Faerie could somehow be salvaged.

## Chapter Two

### Finn

"Ravena does not hate us," I said as I pulled down the old curtains and tossed them in the flames of our backyard bonfire.

"How can she not?" Lochlann dragged out the old lounge, and Rory helped him carry in the new one.

We had known that Ravena would spend her day with Ari, as she almost always did. We could see her from our side windows and knew that Ari would keep her safe. That was one fierce little Fae. I'm grateful Rowan had not applied for her, even though the Queen urged him to. She would have poisoned us all instead of just our brother. We are not good men.

After spending weeks locked in this house, unable to leave, it was only fair that Ravena enjoy some time away from the place. We took advantage of her absence and tossed out every single thing that had been once inside and replaced it with new. Not even the dishes survived our purge. We wanted nothing left to remind ourselves, or Ravena, of the life we lived before she and Ari put Rowan down like a sick animal.

We all knew that's what happened. The whole land did. We didn't care. Not one bit. I'm only happy they chose to spare the three of us, though four deaths would have been impossible to explain. Perhaps we lived by default.

The first time Rowan raped me, I was just a boy, showing no sign of the man I would become. He was a vile creature. Unredeemable. I'd dance on his grave if he had one.

"Ravena does not hate us because her heart is kind. She may not know our history, but she knows we weren't the root of her problems," I said, slipping the new curtains over the rail.

Our old color scheme had been stark, plain, black, and white. Rowan's idea, naturally. Our new scheme was a deep brown and soft blue, similar to the shade of Ravena's skin. Rowan had hated her skin. He said it was one of her many flaws. He did not want blue skinned children and punished her without mercy for the color of her flesh.

I thought she was stunning and flawless. Every shade and every color of the rainbow made her look like a Goddess, but I liked blue best. I hoped she did too. I never wanted to see her wear black again. Never.

"She does not love us." Rory dropped a chair covered in deeper blue fabric by the hearth and stood for a moment, catching his breath. Black hair was plastered to his head from sweat, and he fluffed it out with his hands, his bright blue eyes shining. He was the oldest now and had suffered under Rowan's thumb longer than Lochlann and I.

"She does not know us, only what we have done to her. Give her time. Someday, she will care. We must win her over, that is all."

"How can she care?" Lochlann asked. "After everything, how can she ever want to look at us again?"

"Do you care? For her, I mean?" I asked, jumping from the window to face him.

He stuttered and stumbled an answer, likely knowing where I was heading with my point.

"I care," he answered finally.

"Your history in this house goes back much further than hers. If you can care, she can care. We must give it time." I moved to the next window, jerking the black curtains down and replacing them with another pair of soft blue ones.

Together we worked until the house was remade into something a woman would be proud to call home. When Ravena walked in the door not long before dark and took in the changes, she raised her hand to her mouth in shock. She placed her pale, delicate fingers on every surface, and we could see that she was happy. In the end, that's all we wanted.

She kissed each of us on the lips with such tenderness that I thought I might cry. Maybe we would all find happiness. I would settle for peace if nothing more.

That evening, after dinner and cakes, we sat on benches in the garden and watched the remnants of old things burn.

"Thank you for the house," she said. "It's lovely; it is."

"You're welcome," Lochlann replied with a soft smile.

"This is your home, Ravena. Everything is yours now, including us." I said, watching her watch the low burning fire.

A shudder went through her, and she rose to leave.

"I've caught a bit of a chill; I'm going in." She walked away with her back stiff. She did not look back.

"She hates us," Lochlann repeated his earlier sentiment.

Maybe he was right.

## Chapter Three

### Ravena

"Oh, Goddess. Why can't I just be normal?" I asked. No answer came.

I paced my room until I could pace no more, then grabbed my bathing supplies and walked to the washroom we shared. There was no lock on the door, and I stopped my frantic movements, forcing myself to calm. My heart pounded in my chest, and my breath caught in my throat. Why now?

Why, after their acts of kindness, was I so afraid? Why, after weeks of not even a random touch, was I terrified? I was panicked. I had to restrain myself from pacing some more. Finally, I ran hot water into the tub and sank into it. I poured soap into the running water so that bubbles would cover my nakedness, in case one of them came in.

They had been nothing but kind since I murdered their brother. Would that change after his death had settled in? I couldn't stop thinking about it. My hands shook, my chest pained, and my breath came in gasps. I couldn't understand it.

Forcing myself to breathe, I took each muscle one by one and relaxed it until I was calm. They had never hurt me. Not one on one. In the rare moments, we were allowed to be together unsupervised; they had been nothing but kind.

Finn had once held me all night, not even attempting to lay a finger on me otherwise, at least until Rowan came in and forced himself into me while I slept.

Finn had been so horrified that he tried to pull him off. In his anger, Rowan had taken Finn with his cock and his fists. I watched as tears coursed down his cheeks and his head banged into the wall. Rowan grabbed Finn's neck and choked him as he came. The sight of Finn gasping for air seemed to heighten Rowan's orgasm. I vowed never to allow my actions to cause them to be punished again. It was horrible.

After it was over, he dragged me into his room and beat me until I cried. I didn't have to fake it that night. Had Ari not promised early in our lives to poison any of our mates that mistreated us, I would have snuck out at the earliest opportunity and thrown myself off of the cliff at the crossroads. Fae are hard to kill but not impossible. That cliff is enormous, and the ground is so far below it that mists hide the length of the drop. I would throw myself off more than once, if necessary.

The Consummation Ball was that very night. Rory had some healing magic and was allowed to treat my injuries so that I could be presentable, and that's when Rowan's fate was sealed. Rory's healing was no match for Ari's eyesight. Not even close.

Her fury swept over me like fast moving water, and I knew I would be free.

Only was I?

I washed quickly, dressed in the privacy of the washroom, and raced to my room, pretending the door was locked.

No one accosted me.

# Chapter Four

## Rory

I awoke from sleep, screaming and covered in sweat. Ravena held me tightly, rocking me side to side. She patted my hair and spoke in low tones. I'm not sure what she said, but calmness flowed into me with her words, and I wondered if this was her magic. We never talked about magic. Not in this house.

My breath stuttered in my chest, finally catching. She was damp from her bath and covered head to toe in the soft, purple dressing gown Lochlann had bought for her yesterday. Her heart pounded in her chest, and I wondered how her words could be so calm when her heartbeat was so fast. Only fear causes a heart to pound that way, that, or love. She did not love me.

Pulling me down to her, she cradled me from behind, and I let her. My hearth fire burned bright, and I knew that she must have stoked it. She spoke in her singsong voice until I slept again, erasing the pain from old memories and allowing me to fall into a deep, dreamless sleep.

I am a fighter, known in the land to be among the best. I am also an archer; my arrows fly true and are deadly. Yet there is no fighting an enemy you cannot see, at least not with fists or arrows, and that is all I know. The willowy female brought me peace with her voice, and in this land where there is no freedom, peace is all anyone can hope for.

When I awoke, she was gone. She smells of snow and fresh rain, and her scent lingered on my pillow; I hugged it to me. We would get through this. We had to. Otherwise, the Queen would take her, and Goddess knows where she would go or to whom. There were nightmares in Talamh na Sithe that would beg for one of The Eight.

If we failed in this, we would be punished along with her, and Queen's punishments are possibly worse than Rowan's, though that may not be true.

My brothers and I could not allow that to happen, for we had all suffered enough.

# Chapter Five

## Lochlann

I know she hates me. She is the first woman I ever slept with, and she hates my guts. I can't help but love her. Goddess, but we are a fucked up family.

The first time Rowan told me to touch her was after he had lain with her for the third or fourth time that day. I was so disgusted by him that I didn't think I would be able to perform the act, but I knew that disobeying would make things worse for both of us, so there was no option other than to try.

He sat watching from the corner as I gently lowered myself onto her. I knew she must be sore, but she spread her legs for me and let me in, anyway. I would have faked it if necessary, but my body responded to hers regardless of what my brain thought about the matter. Nothing had ever felt so delicious. She placed her hands on my hips, resting them there lightly, and that simple touch alone had me near finishing.

My only sexual experiences before that moment had been with Rowan, and they had never been enjoyable. Not for me, anyway.

I kissed down her neck, and she gasped softly under my lips. It was likely the only gentleness either of us had ever felt. Although, she would not meet my lips with her own, turning her head and giving me her neck instead.

Inside her, I moved slowly. I didn't know what I was doing, but she seemed to like it. A look of surprise flitted over her face, and she arched into me without thought.

Just as we were about to find release, Rowan ripped me off of her, tossed me aside, and flipped her over. He took her from behind, my seed spilling across her back as she was turned. He said all children would be his, and we were not to come in her. Ever. Under the threat of his punishment, we never did.

He pounded into her, grabbing the back of her neck, bruising her violently, and daring her to complain. She remained silent, and that infuriated him. He liked us to beg and cry. She had not learned that yet, but she would. Quickly.

He dug his nails into the skin on her shoulders, scoring her delicate skin into bloody half moons from his nails. She did cry then.

He came with a roar and smashed her face into the mattress roughly, muffling her sobs. I heard something at that moment that he did not; someone was outside. Someone was listening. There was a startled yelp that was immediately muffled and followed by silence.

The next time I slept with Ravena, Rowan died. I'd say our record together is not very good, but anything leading to his death could not be viewed as a bad thing. Still, I imagined she would hate me forever for what I've done to her.

I lay in bed, reading to fight sleep. I can't sleep in the dark, so a low lamp burned. I heard Rory cry out in another nightmare, something we all suffer from. Ravena was up and out of her room with a rustle of muslin and bare feet and into his in a flash. Her low voice speaking incessantly into the night air until his sobs stopped.

She did not leave his room that I saw, but then I lost the battle with my own nightmares not long after.

How could she still wish to comfort him? What kind of creature survives being tortured and still wishes to ease the pain of others? I didn't understand. Rory had suffered horribly, as had we all, but he suffered earliest and longest from Rowan's abuse. With his soft features and pretty looks, Finn had suffered the worst but for the least amount of time and seemed not to be as touched by the darkness as Rory. Something in him had broken and would likely never be fixed.

As ashamed as I was over the years of not standing up to Rowan for myself, I was more ashamed of not standing up to him for my brothers. Although, my deepest shame is that I did not stand up to him for Ravena. In time, he would have broken her, and I would have done nothing. Instead, a diminutive, red-haired, and not very Fae like Fae ended the madness for us. I am forever grateful to her.

Would Ravena recover? After only a few weeks of suffering in our house, I hoped so. I suppose the bigger question was, after a lifetime of it, could we?

## Chapter Six

### Ravena

When I slipped from Rory's room and back into my own, dawn had just breached the horizon. I was tired. Despite the new furnishings and comforting change of the place, the house still held onto memories no house should.

We should burn it.

I dressed quickly in a pale yellow dress and slid thin house pants underneath it for added comfort. Why dresses have ever been acceptable for women to wear, I will never understand. They provide too easy access for cruel men. Rowan had never allowed me to wear pants.

I headed for the door and Ari's bakery. I would get breakfast for the others before they woke up and say hello to my sister at the same time.

"Good morning, sister," she greeted me as I walked through her door.

"Good morning. Hello, Seal," I added at the large man scowling at everything, including the helpless cupcakes.

"You look well, Ravena." He inclined his head to me and turned his darkening scowl to Ari. "Be cautious with your

19

friend, Ari. The Queen does not need to become any more suspicious than she already is. She could move you if she chooses."

"Don't worry about that, Seal. Now off you go." She handed him a basket and stood on her tiptoes to kiss his chin. He glowered some more then slipped out the door, eyeing us as he went like we might be dangerous. Ha. Ari and I dangerous?

Possibly.

When Seal was gone, Ari gripped me to her, hugging herself to me. She came to the tops of my breasts, so it was hard for her to surround me as she was trying to do. She pushed me away.

"Are you well? Are things better? If any of the rest of them need to go, I will do it. Families have heart conditions; perhaps, they share Rowan's weakness." She sat me at a table and shoved a plate of muffins and a pot of tea under my face.

"No, they are fine, I swear, Ari. They have suffered enough and are glad he is gone. We tiptoe around one another, jumping at shadows. They were innocents in this. They've suffered far worse than I. Is your mate always so scowly?" I picked at a muffin.

"Yes. Seal is quite often scowly, but under the scowls, he is a sweet thing. Do you like them? The other three?" she asked, her voice lowering to a whisper.

"They are not unkind. Rowan was as bad, or worse, to them. Time will tell about the rest. Rowan's cruelty may have damaged them irreparably." Ari's face froze in a smile, and she looked over my shoulder.

"Come, Lochlann, join us," she said, and I turned in time to see his fractured eyes drop. He stepped back through the door as Ari approached him. It was odd to see such a large man step away from such a tiny individual.

"I will tell you this once, Lochlann, as long as my friend is safe in your home, you have nothing to fear from me. My word to you." She held his eyes for a moment.

He stepped inside the door but just, and watched as Ari turned her back to him to make him a plate of muffins. "Sit." She placed the plate on the table. Lochlann sat.

"You must be careful of the face you present to the Queen. She is more dangerous than ever. Should she think your union is not a good one, she will move you, sister. Sometimes the enemy known is better than the enemy not. Tread with care. She came to our home and searched it for poison," Ari stopped at my sharp intake of breath. "She found nothing. It was moved by my mates before I could hide it," she finished with a dark grin. Lochlann's eyes rounded. I have seen the face of Ari's protectiveness many times. Few others have. It is fierce, stunning, and more than a little frightening.

"They know?"

"Everyone knows. No one has proof. Thanks to Lochlann for witnessing the unfortunate event firsthand and verifying there was no foul play." She sat back in her chair and eyed him from across the table.

"I will never tell my Lady. It would mean death to us all as accomplices, and I have no wish to die now that I am finally free of him."

Ari seemed satisfied with his statement and let his eyes go.

Her bloodline can lie freely, by some freak of Fae magic, but only hers. The rest of us can twist the truth, making you believe a different one, but we cannot lie. His direct statement would be considered both a truth and a promise; he left no room for variance. She nodded at him, rising to fill a basket. She handed it to me when she was done.

"Make your mating a happy one, if you can. I try to deflect the Queen's attention from the rest of you as much as possible, but you are interesting to her right now. Don't be interesting. Be happy if you can, but be boring and uninteresting as diligence necessitates if you cannot.

"She mentioned in her visit that she wants to replace Rowan with another. Any man she places in your home could be a spy. Don't give her a reason to do this." Ari leaned into us, and ferocity flowed from her.

She would be Queen. All of The Eight knew it. Her magic was powerful even in this dead place, and she hadn't even reached the peak of it yet. Many a long, cold winter's night was spent huddled in bed, fighting to stay warm and listening to Ari's plans to challenge her mother for the throne.

No one doubted her.

She hated her mother, and her mother hated her. Proof of that was everywhere, in every deed done and move the Queen made. I wondered why she allowed her to live at all. It was a curious thing.

Ari would be Queen, though, and I, for one, looked forward to seeing her on the throne. Lochlann placed a tentative hand on my back and guided me out of the bakery and back into our home.

Worried eyes fixed on us as we walked through the door. Lochlann said nothing as I sat the basket on the table and pulled out muffins and tea for all. The others waited like frightened animals, unable to approach and ready to run.

Ari was right. We had to fix this, or the Queen would deem the contract broken and fix it for us. I took a deep breath and put a smile on my face.

It would be up to me. I could see that. I liked a challenge, and this presented one. How to fix three broken males? I didn't know but was going to find out and do what I could.

"Eat breakfast before you leave for work. I'm going to change and go plant some flowers." The look of shock that swept through their faces was slowly replaced by something happier, something that looked almost like hope.

## Chapter Seven

### Finn

"She's going to plant flowers," I said as we walked towards the center of town, where we would split. Rory is an archer and would go where his Captain asked him. Lochlann is an infantryman and would likely have drills. I would go to my studio for the first time in more seasons than I could count.

I hadn't made art of any kind since before Ravena came to us, and even afterward, it wasn't in me to find beauty in the world.

"She says she is going to plant flowers," Lochlann grumbled. "What does that mean?"

"It means, brother, that she is trying to settle. Flowers are a beautiful thing, and only happy people grow them. To nourish a flower is to nourish the beauty one sees in the world. It's a positive sign." I tilted my face to the sun and let the warmth flow through me.

Ravena didn't hate us. If a person's heart is filled with hate, they do not plant flowers. I smiled at my brothers and wished them farewell as we went our separate ways.

I jammed the key in the lock and pushed my shoulder into the door of my shop. Dust had settled on every surface, and rats scurried as I moved to light torches and collect wood for the fires.

Glass lay in various stages of finish on just about every surface. My creativity had waned over the years until I stopped making the beautiful blown glass I was known for and started making more utilitarian items like dishes. My medium changed too, from delicate, brightly colored glass to clay.

My shop was a mess.

It was one of those messes that overwhelm you to look at, and I almost walked back out the door, locking it behind me forever. Instead, I began to sort through items, tossing those away that I no longer saw life in and setting those aside I did.

By midday, my shop was spotless and warm from the fire. By evening the first glass piece I made in many, many seasons lay on my counter. As the only glassmith left in the land, it filled me with pride to look upon the little bird I had made. She was delicate and refined, but in her core, you sensed a greater strength. The glass would be unbreakable; it was my magic. I could make anything out of the medium, and it could not be destroyed.

Somewhere along the way, I had lost this. Lost myself, lost my magic, and given up on beauty. I placed the bird in my pocket. Its slightly blue coloration and inner fire reminded me of Ravena. I would give it to her later. Maybe I would help her plant flowers.

Life is a funny thing, and I was just beginning to realize it. We were entering a new season, all of us together. We would fail or win as a whole, not as individuals. While our pasts were dark and filled with pain, the future did not have to be.

I held the unbreakable glass bird in my hand for most of the day. She was a symbol of a new season to come. A beginning yet to flesh out. I would not give up on that.

I walked home early in the afternoon and found the house tidy. I went through the front door and out the back, leaving the keys to my shop on the counter. Our tall, slender Ravena bent over one of the flowerbeds in the garden. Spring flowers bloomed from pots and hangers everywhere. Our house had been transformed into a magical place filled with sweet smells and bright colors in half a day. I wondered if it was her magic.

A red flowerpot filled with the brightest red flowers I have ever seen sat on the garden wall. It seemed oddly out of place but beautiful nonetheless. Sprigs of herbs had been set in a planter under the kitchen window, and everywhere I looked, something bloomed and grew. It was magnificent.

Ravena stood, straightening her back and placing a muddied hand on it to push at sore muscles. I went to her and placed my hands slowly on her shoulders, waiting for her to relax before I set about kneading the knots I found there.

"You've been busy. It's magnificent," I whispered as I applied steady pressure to the sore spots I found.

"Thank you. I lost track of time and didn't make dinner." She dropped her chin to her neck and let out a soft moan when I massaged the base of it.

Rowan would have lost his mind had she not had dinner ready for him when he returned home, and I wondered if she was testing me.

"I don't care about dinner, Ravena. You've done too much as it is. We can make something or go to the diner and eat there," I said, allowing no part of my body to touch her but my hands. She was a horrible cook anyway, but I would never tell her that

She turned in my arms, tilting her head to mine. I was tall but not gigantic like my brothers. Ravena's head came to the bottom of my chin; her lips were within reach of mine. I froze, dropping my hands to my sides.

"It's okay, Finn." She stretched up enough to brush my lips with hers before slipping her tongue between them, urging me to kiss her.

I reached around, placing a hand on the small of her back. She didn't melt into me, but she didn't pull away, either. Her body touched mine lightly. I let her kiss me, returning it cautiously but unwilling to push the kiss. I didn't know how to do this. Any of it. When she finished, she pulled away, walking inside.

I heard the water run for a long time after and wondered what it all meant.

## Chapter Eight

## Lochlann

I came home to find a paradise in place of the house I left that morning. Ravena sat on the chaise reading; her black hair lay long and wet down her back. She dropped her book, jumping to her feet.

"Stop. Don't get up," I said.

Finn sat by the fire, staring into the orange flames with a look of deep contemplation on his face.

"I didn't make anything," she said, stumbling over her words and worrying her lower lip while casting nervous glances at Finn.

"You don't need to make dinner. You've done enough, anyway. The house looks beautiful; thank you." I edged toward her but stopped short. I kept the smile on my face by sheer will. It made me sad that she thought she would be punished for not cooking a meal for us.

In her mind, she must be terrified. She has known nothing but pain since she came to this house, and no amount of painting or new furniture can fix the damage Rowan did. That we all did. Time would fix it, maybe, but until then, I didn't want her to be afraid to be here. "You don't ever have to cook; not if you don't want to, we've cooked for ourselves for years. It's up to you. Okay?"

"Okay," she sank back down and the chaise and reached for her book, still unsure. "Will you sit with me?" she asked, her eyes lingering on mine.

Her question took me by surprise. I moved slowly to sit next to her, being careful not to touch her. She brought her legs under herself, tucking them in. Her toes just barely brushed my thigh.

"What are you reading?" I asked. Finn had turned from staring at the fire and was now watching us with rapt attention.

"*The History and Origin of the Races and Their Connection with the Goddess*," she answered quietly.

"So just light reading then," I laughed, feeling my smile crinkle the edges of my eyes.

"Yes, exactly." She laughed too, and the sound warmed my heart. It was like a thousand little bells tinkling in my ears.

"Would you like me to get a job? I could work at the nursery; I'm quite good with plants." Her smile faded a bit, the remnants hugging her lips as if unwilling to go completely.

"If you want, you can, although you don't need to work. You can do anything you like. You're not a prisoner here." I turned to face her full on, and her smile dropped away.

"Not anymore," she whispered.

"Never again, Ravena. I swear it." I felt the promise settle between us.

"I will think on it." She arranged herself so that her legs were tucked under the opposite hip, her side resting against mine.

She picked up her book again while we awaited Rory's arrival.

As she read, her face moved expressively. I realized at that moment how intelligent she was. Origins is an in-depth book on how all the Fae races started as one before diverging into each distinct, different branch of the family tree.

I considered myself reasonably intelligent, but she flipped through pages much faster than I ever could, and her face registered every fact she read. Odd that I hadn't seen it before.

Finn watched her from the corner of his eyes, and I knew this information was registering with him as well. Finn was undoubtedly the smartest of the four of us brothers, despite what Rowan thought. I had never seen such intelligence in him, not like what shined in the face of our willowy, lovely mate.

It's not that I underestimated her. I'm not sure I thought about it at all. I'm not sure I saw her as an individual with different thoughts, traits, or strengths until that moment. I vowed then to learn more about her and see her as a unique and independent person.

It's interesting how one moment in the span of a thousand can change so much and greatly influence the many that follow. I leaned into her just a bit as she read, loving the way her side rose and fell against mine as she breathed. I knew then that I was hers.

Rory came home not long after, stopping short at the domestic scene that greeted him. He was later than usual, but not much past sunset. I had intended to make something for us all to eat, but the feel of Ravena against my side dissuaded me from rising.

"Rory, glad you finally made it," Finn said, jumping up from his spot by the fire. "Let's go and grab a bite unless you're too tired."

Rory stood, looking confused. He gazed around the room, then back into the coming darkness. I had never seen him look so unsure, like maybe he walked into the wrong house. He slid sideways through the entrance, not coming in all the way and not leaving either. I watched him take in the flowers and saw his nose tip up and scent the fresh, clean scent of the house. His gaze lingered on Ravena, curled up comfortably next to me.

"Ok. Dinner." He backed step by step out of the door, watching as we rose to follow.

# Chapter Nine

## Rory

I walked into the wrong fucking house. I had to lean back and check the front of the place to be sure this was my home, but even that didn't assure me I was in the right place as the exterior now flowed over with flowers. Bright things, red, yellow, purple, white, and orange blooms had come from nowhere and taken root in the few short hours I was gone. I didn't even understand what was happening.

Ravena lay curled like a cat against Lochlann, and Finn jumped up from the fire like he'd been caught doing something he shouldn't. Which would be what exactly? A deep sense of calm permeated the air in the house. It must have made Finn jumpy.

I stepped back through the doorway, shaking my head and wondering if maybe I was dreaming. Perhaps I had stepped into another realm on the way home. Those places exist. I know it. A place where nothing bad had ever happened in this house, and the people living in it were a family.

The others caught up to me. Ravena's fingers brushed mine before grabbing them and holding onto them a little tighter than was probably normal. Whatever normal was. Warmth spread up my arm as her hand grasped mine, slipping across my chest and into my gut like the ember of a fire, and I wondered again what was happening. It was like my broken family had been replaced while I was at work, and I was the only one to notice.

We walked to the place a few doors down from Ari's darkened bakery that served meals well into the night for those men without mates to cook for them at home, which was just about everyone in the land. Not that I cared if Ravena cooked. To be honest, she wasn't very good at it anyway.

As we walked in the door, the place went silent, all eyes turning to us. Chairs scooted away from the only empty table as others made way for us and watched with speculative eyes. Rowan was known for his cruelty. As an extension of him, that label had been placed on us as well, although we had done nothing to earn it.

Ravena chatted, her face brilliant with animation, not seeming to notice how silent the place had become. She swung my hand once in hers before pulling her fingers away and flopping down in the chair Lochlann held out for her. I growled low in warning in case any of the men had ideas and watched in wonder as eyes darted away immediately.

Maybe Rowan's reputation in this instance was not a bad thing. Undoubtedly, many of the men here would love to take our willowy, blue skinned Fae off our hands. That wasn't happening. She'd paid her debt to the land if ever there had been one. She was done being tormented by Talamh na Sithe, and if that meant I had to become my brother to keep her safe, then so be it.

Conversations slowly wound around us until the place was once again loud and boisterous. A serving girl brought ale and menus. I watched as Ravena sipped her drink, something she had never been allowed to have in our home. A look of slow rapture slipped across her face, and she took a second sip, her lips curling upwards into a soft smile. She caught me staring. "This is so good," she said, sipping again.

"Sip slowly, little bird; it sneaks up on you." I laughed, really laughed, as she took a long pull on her ale, her eyes already going misty. We'd be carrying the lass out of here for sure.

"I'm not little," she said, cocking her brow at me. My own narrowed in confusion. Something had happened. Something I missed.

"You are little to me. Maybe not to Ari or the small brown skinned girl with the red hair, but to me, you are little, little bird." My lip quirked up in what might have been a smile.

"Teagan," she said, eyeing me as she took another pull on her ale. "Her name is Teagan."

"Whatever her name is doesn't matter. Your name is the only one we knew." I said.

"I see. What of Ari? I know the Queen wanted you to take her."

I barked a laugh then, the sound so unfamiliar to me that it came out coarse and broken. The room got quiet again.

"Yes, we knew her name, I suppose, but that is not a fire we wanted to stoke. She's crazy. Even Rowan was leery of her, and no one wanted to be tied to the Queen like that. Her mates need their heads examined." I smiled at her, trying to get it to reach my eyes. It almost made it, but not quite.

"She is my sister; you hush about her." She kicked me under the table with her little foot. "What are you having?" she asked, peeking at me over her menu.

"I think I will have the back strap of stag," I answered, watching her. She leaned to me, idly pushing a strand of black hair off of my face.

"How about you?" she asked Lochlann.

"Broasted Sea Monster," he answered, not looking up at her.

Her eyes went impossibly wide, and she scanned the menu fervently before hitting him with it. The room went silent again. "There is no such thing as broasted sea monster, Sir. What is broasted anyway? You made that up."

"Mermaid then."

"You are not eating mermaid." Her voice lilted up an octave, and she began to ignore him. "How about you, Finn?"

"Why do you ask, love," he said, his voice loud enough to be heard throughout the place. He didn't look at her, or any of us for that matter, as he said those words so casually, and I realized something then. We were playing parts here. This was some play that I had not read the script to. I didn't understand, not really, but I knew word of this night would reach the Queen. The implications of these interactions were not hard to understand.

"What are you having?" I asked.

"I'm not sure; everything looks so good that I want to try it all."

"Then we will each order something different so that you can." I smiled down at her, even as I scowled over her head and met the eyes of every single person in the room. Every. Single. One.

Ravena drank another ale and ate most of her plate and half of each of ours. She was so thin that I wasn't sure where she put it all. Her belly was rounded under her hand when she rose with a groan. I knew she wasn't pregnant, but the little swell of her food baby made her look that way. It was cute.

She wobbled a bit, lurching into Finn with a soft gasp. "I think it snuck up on me, it did." Her words slurred just a bit.

Lochlann tried to help right her, but she teetered to me, a large grin splashed across her face.

"Gods, who ordered her that last ale?" I asked. No one answered. Picking up the stumbling woman, I tossed her over my shoulder, placing a light smack on her ass. Nothing painful, nothing that would even sting, just a small warning that came with a growl. "Be still, Ravena, stop wiggling."

She howled laughter even as I felt her tremble at such a light smack. I hated it. But if we wanted talk about us in this town to settle and speculation on the Queen's part to cease, then I would perform the final act in the play to the best of my ability. I swept through the door with Ravena over my shoulder. She patted each of my butt checks in time to a song I did not hear, and I wondered for the millionth time what the fuck was happening.

# Chapter Ten

## Ravena

Oh my head, I thought as I rolled over on my bed. What had I drank last night? Rory warned me. He did. At least he tried. In some attempt to celebrate my freedom, I had drunk two ales that kicked like a horse. A giant's horse. I was never drinking again.

It felt like I was sucking on a small, furry woodland creature; my mouth was so dry. I flopped myself upright, stumbling into the washroom. The world tilted, or maybe I did. Something tilted. I splashed my face with water and drank deeply from the sink.

They had tossed me on my bed in my clothes and bolted, no doubt. I didn't blame them. All I remember is that my laughter was too loud and likely embarrassing to them. Ugh. What did I do? I stripped out of my clothes and rinsed off with cold water in the metal bathing tub. Wrapping myself in a towel, I stepped out into the hallway and headed back to my room.

Soft light shone from underneath Lochlann's closed door. I hesitated before knocking softly.

"Yes?" His voice was muffled with sleep; he must have fallen asleep with his light on.

"Sorry for waking you. I just wanted to apologize for, uh, whatever I did tonight." I put my hand on his door before turning to walk away.

"You can come in," he said. I paused, straightening my back. I was sober now, mostly.

Later I would blame it on the ale running through my blood, but that isn't true. I had resolved to fix this situation, and Lochlann was the first step. Steeling my shoulders, I turned and walked back to his door, opening it and closing it behind me.

I stood in his room, wrapped in only a towel. His eyebrows flew to his hairline when I dropped it. I walked slowly to his bed, easing down beside him, then slowly moving to mount his lap with the covers between us. I let my fingers trail over his bare chest. His face was lined from the linens where he had slept on it. There wasn't a book in sight or a reason for his torches to be lit that I could see, and it made me wonder if he could sleep with them out.

My fingertips traced the smooth lines of his lips, and I took him all in. His eyes were a darker blue, like the deepest parts of a lake. They were so dark as almost to match his hair, but they were blue all the same.

His full lips twitched as I studied him. His hair was short, but there was just enough on the top that I could slide my fingers through it. Black scruff covered his face, but his neck was shaved clean. He didn't sport a beard, but he often forgot to shave long enough to allow this rough shadow to grow. The straight line of his jaw blended perfectly with the strong muscles in his neck. He was not pretty, not like Finn, but Goddess was he gorgeous. Striking really. His teeth were so white and straight, just a hint of them gleamed through his parted lips.

I stared at him with intense fixation. I couldn't help it.

Under my hands, he did not move; he did not breathe. I felt him rise under the covers and twitch against my sex, but his hands did not reach for me.

He watched me explore him with my eyes and hands. I leaned over him tentatively, placing my lips in the hollow under his ears before kissing down his neck and up the other side. I met his lips with mine, keeping my eyes open to watch his reaction. I could see he wasn't sure of this.

Not sure of me.

Only when I rose up to remove the blankets from his hips did he touch me. He traced the curve of my side down to my hip, resting his hands there. My tongue slipped in between his lips. I brought my hands to his chest and rolled my core against him, dipping my head at the sensation growing in between my hips. I felt heavy in places I didn't understand.

His hand moved to my chin, raising my face to his. I had been staring at that part of me, touching that part of him, and I couldn't look away from it.

"You can stop, Ravena," he said, his voice cracking with need.

"Do you want me to?" I asked.

"Gods no," he said, resting his head back against the headboard, his eyes closed. I kissed up his neck again and felt wetness pooling between us. I had never been wet like this.

Lifting again, I gripped his shaft with my hand and slid onto him. A gasp came from me when I had him seated in the deepest part of me, and still, more wetness flowed. I stayed like that, watching his face.

His hands rested, still and unmoving on my hips. His eyes were closed, and his face tight with strain; I could feel his cock twitch inside me. I rose over him again and slid down, bringing a soft moan from him. I moved again, faster. Kissing his lips as I rode him. I had never been in this position before; it was a position of great power. Every tilt of my hips and every stroke of my body brought guttural noises I had never heard from him. I went fast, and then I went slow, exploring what each different move might do and how they might feel. Finally, I found the pace where friction was the sweetest, and I rode him hard chasing what? I did not know but chasing something.

His eyes were open now and firmly locked onto my face. I had never had an orgasm. I knew they existed but had not experienced one. My body started to tremble of its own accord. My nipples rubbed his chest and hardened to stones against him. Still, his hands did not leave my hips, fingers now digging into the flesh there and holding my hips tight.

From nowhere, it came, starting in that heavy place and spreading out like an ocean. My body took over, tilting and writhing on his cock to bring me to the highest point, and when it crested, I went over, taking any coherent thoughts I once had with it. I shattered on him, my body violently squeezing his to the point of delirium, and I felt him stretch me wider as an orgasm hit him too. My muscles clenched around him, drawing more and more spasms from him until he lay spent and empty underneath me.

I kissed across his face, rose from the bed to blow the torches out, then snuggled into him in the dark, wrapping my arms around him to pull him to me. I was asleep in moments.

## Chapter Eleven

## Lochlann

I couldn't believe I was still alive. I thought for sure when she came to me that I would be dead within the hour. Fear had paralyzed me, but still, I gave my consent. If she wanted to kill me, I would not stop her. If she wanted to kill me, it would not be a bad way to go. Even my bastard of a brother had a smile on his face when he died.

She lay curled next to me, soft smile on her pretty face, and the occasional satisfied sigh that came from her cut me with razor soft precision. I didn't feel the pain from it until the blood was already flowing. Goddess, but she came beautifully, her face twisted by the hands of passion was even more lovely. She had never come before. Not that I saw. Not that I knew. Rowan would not have allowed it; I have no doubt.

Why?

Why now?

I had so many questions for the sweet girl that smelled like sex, snow, and fresh rain, but I would not ask them. I would enjoy this moment. Never had I come like that. Never. I wanted to do it again. Right now, but after her experiences in this house, I felt like I should not. At least not until she brought her leg over my hip, brushing it across my stiffening cock. Something in me broke, and I turned her, burying my face between her legs and causing her to give a startled cry and momentarily scrabble away from me. I placed my hand on her gently, saying her name.

She calmed under it, stilling. None of us had ever done this to her, but it came to me with the natural flow of ideas of the many things I wanted to experience. I wanted to taste her. That she also tasted of me made it better. Our fluids mingled like the perfect, sweet frosting on one of her friend's cupcakes. I lapped at her until she was clean from it, circling my tongue on that spot that men talk about.

She bucked away from me, but I wrapped my arms around her legs and dragged her back, laving that hard nub until her legs trembled in my arms.

Reaching up, I smoothed a hand across the peak of her nipple, feeling the hard bud of it like a rose that hasn't yet bloomed. She arched, bringing herself deeper onto my face. I groaned into her sweetness, flicking that center with my tongue until she screamed out my name. Clear fluid poured from her, and I licked it up as fast as it flowed. Nothing had ever tasted better.

One more time, she cried out, grunting and grabbing for me, pulling me up to her and guiding my cock into her. She clenched around me as I pushed in, then clenched some more as I caused her orgasm to deepen with my thrusts. I did that. Me. It was an incredible feeling.

I never knew that sex could bring anything other than pain, but there we were. Both of us caught in the moment. For all the restraint I showed earlier when I thought she was fucking me to death, I gave her the opposite now. I touched her everywhere. Every part of her, her face, her breasts, her neck, everywhere.

The hollow of her throat held the moonlight like a cup, the blush of her nipples was like a pink flower preparing to bloom, her skin was so soft that I could get lost in it, and her scent drove me mad. I had never needed anything more. She was like oxygen, and I knew I would die without her.

I kissed her deeply, twining my tongue with hers and taking her moans into me. I could live off of them for days. This was everything. She was everything.

I reached between us and flicked that part of her that I did not know what to call, but I touched it until she writhed like a mad thing, causing my cock only to get harder. She called my name and shook underneath me, her fingers digging into the muscles on my arms, holding me tight, wild eyes catching mine. If I died with my name on her lips, then the Goddess does hear our prayers because never had I felt more whole. Complete.

Unable to help it, I slammed into her until I came with an animal noise. It flowed from some ancient depth, and I dropped onto her, my heart pounding in my ears and against her chest.

And still, I lived.

I pushed off of her in horror.

"I'm sorry. Goddess, I am so sorry, Ravena." I looked at her with horror filled eyes.

"For what, Lochlann?" she asked, her confused eyes roaming my face. Fingers trailed down my chest. She snuggled into me, taking in the scent of our pleasure. "That was amazing. Thank you."

I jerked back like I was slapped. She adjusted herself around me, unaware of my confusion. I draped my arm over her and settled into her peace. Within moments she was snoring quietly, and I was staring at her in stunned silence. I stared at her for hours until sleep finally took me too. I didn't even notice that my room was dark, dark for the first time since I was a child.

## Chapter Twelve

## Ravena

I awoke to the feel of strong arms behind me, pulling me close. My head ached lightly, and my body was sore in places it had never been before. It was a soreness brought by pleasure and not by pain. I swear my uterus hurt from how many times I came last night. I smiled to myself, feeling the soft hairs of Lochlann's arms tickle across my lips.

Peace was possible. Peace in this house was also possible, but what about love? I had never dreamed that would exist for me. I could see it as a possibility now, not right now, but maybe someday. Today I would settle for this. Sighing, I closed my eyes again.

Sunlight peeked into the windows, and I knew we should get up. The men had work, and I planned to speak with the nursery owner in town. With my magic, I could make things grow. Flowers, vegetables, trees, whatever would flourish with my touch. Although I wanted for nothing, I would not mind having money to trade for goods on my own, not that they wouldn't give it to me. I would enjoy having something to do other than wait at home for the men to return. I wanted some measure of independence.

Rory and Finn's voices reached me through the closed door. It opened slowly, and Lochlann reared up and threw a pillow at them. The door shut.

"Are you alive, Lochlann?" Rory demanded.

"Of course I'm alive, you ass." Lochlann turned me to him and kissed my face before releasing me and rising.

They thought I had killed him.

Like I did Rowan.

No wonder the poor man was so paralyzed the first time. Living through that made him bold. I chuckled as I rose, too, grabbing my towel. As Lochlann dressed, I opened the door, letting my fingers trail over Rory's chest on my way to the washroom. I felt the light blush creep up my cheeks as he turned and watched me walk away from him.

I washed off and dressed in pants and a loose shirt. Gathering my hair at the nape of my neck, I pulled it into a tail, tying it with a blue ribbon. I took a moment to brush a light powder over my nose and apply just a hint of lip stain.

When Rowan lived, I was not allowed to wear makeup. He called it frippery. Only the night of the consummation ball was I allowed to wear it, and that was to cover the bruises he had caused the night before. I would test his brothers' thoughts on this a little at a time.

In the kitchen, the men gathered over tea. Someone had made eggs and brought out salted meat and butter. A bowl of fruit rested on the table, and I helped myself to a little of everything. I enjoyed eating. I could do it all day. Fortunately, genetics had gifted me with the ability to eat like a Troll and stay slim as a willow. I was grateful.

Rory and Finn watched me carefully. I made sure to stay light and happy with them. They needed fixing, and I would do it. I needed this to work; I did not want to start over someplace else.

Peace starts with a state of mind. All things do. Want peace? Engage it, call for it, live it, and it will come. The same with misery. Pain is caused. Peace is found. It can be found in the wings of a butterfly or the fragrance of a flower. It can be found anywhere, and I would find it here. We all would. Brick by brick, layer by layer, I would live the life I wanted until it was real and built around me in such a sturdy way as to never be broken down.

I kissed each of the men, in turn, letting my lips linger over theirs. I sent them on their way with confused looks and soft smiles. Once they were gone, I went about straightening up the house and cleaning up any lingering mess. I touched my plants and watched their blooms grow. Outside I touched the vegetables in our garden. Even though it was very early in the Fae spring, they flourished, oblivious to the nightly chill.

I replaced the flowers on the tables and changed Lochlann's sheets. They were dry and crusted with our combination of juices. I loved it. Bringing a man to lose control like that? I had never felt more powerful. One down, two to go. Feeling more confident than I ever had, I walked across to say hello to Ari before heading on to the nursery to look for work.

It was a lovely place. Green plants dripped and flowed over every surface. Trees and flowers bloomed, and the air was filled with the scent of them. I walked the rows under the roof made of glass so that even winter sun would nourish them. I reached out with my senses and felt them grow, felt their health and their needs.

Given the chance, I would touch them all. First, I would get the job.

"Can I help you?" I turned to find a smallish silver haired male watching me, his face thoughtful.

"My name is Ravena, and I was wondering if you needed some part-time help?"

"I know who you are, Miss Ravena. You're Rory's mate." His voice was quiet, higher-pitched, and almost feminine.

Most people thought of me as Rowan's mate or Rowan's possession. It was the first time someone had mentioned any of the other men to me in that context; it was curious. I tilted my head and answered, "I am. I am also very good with plants. It's part of my magic."

He watched me. His expression contained something I couldn't understand, but it looked almost like hostility. He closed his eyes, taking a deep breath. "I could use the help, I suppose." He gave me a small smile that didn't quite reach his eyes. "You're pretty. I guess I knew you would be. Rory said you were; his description didn't do you justice."

"Thank you," I said. His gaze was so intense that I looked away from him, choosing instead to walk around and start touching the plants. I let them take from my magic what they needed. "What is your name, Sir, if you are to be my boss?"

"Call me Elic. You can come for two days a week to start, four in a fortnight. We will see how it goes after that." His shoulders slumped a little, and I wondered what he was about.

"Are you friends with Rory?" I asked, moving on to the next row of plants and letting my fingers graze over them slowly.

"In a manner of speaking, I suppose," he answered, his eyes following my every move.

"Well, that's good. He needs all the friends and people who care about him that he can get. His family has been through a lot." I smiled at him fully.

This small Fae loved Rory; it radiated off of him. Heartbreak lined his face, and a hint of jealousy glinted in his eyes. I would ask Rory about it later. It would be important to know if the feelings were mutual or unrequited. Rory and I had been together sexually but not fully.

My memories of those times were overshadowed by Rowan. Rowan was all consuming in those moments and every other, but Rory didn't strike me as a man who only wanted other men. I decided it would be best to find out before I moved on with my plans for him.

"I thank you for the opportunity to work with you. When would you like me to start?" I asked, moving back to stand in front of him. His delicate features and silver hair were striking in the light coming through the glass.

"It seems you've already started; you've touched all the pants and made them grow." Finally, his smile reached his yellow eyes. They were lovely and went with his coloring to make him quietly stunning. "If you water them and check for weeds, you can consider this day one. I will pay you daily in case it doesn't work out.

"Sounds fair; thank you again." I turned from him and wandered into the nursery. The smell of damp earth and plant life settled into my soul, making me happy. I took a watering can and went plant by plant and row by row, watering them all and pulling weeds that might be growing.

Elic moved quietly around me throughout the day, showing customers various plants and flowers they might want. I got some curious glances but was otherwise left alone.

As the sun was setting, I heard Finn's voice from the front of the building. He spoke softly to Elic, placing his hand on the other man's shoulder, trying to ease the look of distress on his face. They looked over at me and started when they saw I was staring at them.

I wiped my hands on my apron and removed it, placing it on a nail to dry. Smoothing my shirt, I walked to the two men.

"I came to walk you home, love. Are you ready?"

"Yes, I think so. It was a good day, Elic."

"It was. You do lovely work." He held out a small bag of coins. I took it, sliding it into my pants pocket. "Will you be back in a day or so?"

"I will." I turned from him stiffly. Finn placed his hand on the small of my back, guiding me out.

## Chapter Thirteen

### Finn

"Is there something about Elic that I should know, Finn?" Ravena asked when we were far enough away from the big greenhouse so as not to be overheard.

Sighing, I grabbed her fingers and tugged at them. I didn't want to answer, but I needed to. "He and Rory had a relationship."

"Oh. Ok. I. I wish I had known before I went there asking for a job," she said, slanting her beautiful blue eyes to mine. "I mean, that's not at all unusual, but it would have been good to know. I suppose that explains why he looked at me strangely all day."

"Elic loves Rory. He has for a very long time. They kept their relationship a secret, but Rowan found out about it and lost his shit," I said, pulling her to a bench along the main road through town. We sat down, quartered to one another. She was so patient as she waited for more, but I saw a hint of worry in the way her eyes pinched at the corners.

I continued, "Rowan almost beat Rory to death. Rory has always liked other males. He had never been with a female until you. I honestly don't know which way his affections lie now," I stopped and watched as her face fell.

"I see," she said, staring at her folded hands.

"I don't think you do. Rory hid his relationships from Rowan; we all did. Rowan wanted us to himself and hated the idea of sharing. He was brutal about it. Rory is a fighter and a hell of an archer. He is incredibly strong and tough, but Rowan could beat him in any fight.

"When Rowan found out about Elic, He beat Rory, leaving him for dead. The only reason he didn't die was that Elic found him. You would think that Elic would have plant magic, but he is as strong a mender as the land knows. He worked on Rory, but after that, he said they couldn't be together anymore. It just wasn't worth the risk to him." I took Ravena's birdlike hand in my own. Her delicate fingers smoothed my own.

"I don't know what to do with this information, Finn. I had hoped to make a home with all of you, but if Rory doesn't want that, well, I don't know how to proceed. It scares me." Her face paled, and she looked at me with panic in her eyes.

"Rory wants a home. We all do. These days with you have been the best we have ever had. Regardless of Rory's other desires, that will not change." I did my best to make her feel that her place in our home was secure, but she was right. Should Rory attempt to move on and away from his mating with her and his home with us all, the Queen would take her for sure. Two men would not be enough to satisfy Aramea's genetic desires.

"I wish I had known before." Her whisper was almost too low to hear. "I must try with him, Finn. I must."

"I know. We all must. That's all we can do." She rose; keeping my hand in hers, we walked through town, taking our time.

It wasn't a bad place, not really. It would have been beautiful if it didn't always seem to hold the edge of death. What would this land be like touched by the laughter of children? What could this land be without such a harsh ruler? I hoped for change and thought that maybe someday it would come.

The evening sun was setting, and torches had been lit to chase darkness from the town center. The night was cooling at a rapid pace, and goosebumps dotted Ravena's neck. I wrapped her in my arms, enjoying our silence.

We walked through the door to our house together. The smell of fresh bread and spiced meat assaulted my nose, and my stomach growled in desperation. I had forgotten I was hungry.

My shop had been busy. The Fae were happy to have their glassmaker back and eager to own a small piece of my magic. I had not eaten since I grabbed a muffin at Ari's bakery this morning.

Ravena's stomach growled an answer, and I doubted she had eaten all day either. She hadn't planned on staying at the greenhouse, and I doubted she took any kind of break. She moved through the house like a specter, eyes missing nothing.

Lochlann and Rory talked in the kitchen; they placed food on plates and ale in mugs when they saw us enter.

"I should clean up," Ravena said, skirting by the furniture, heading back to the washroom.

"Eat first," Lochlann came and pulled her into his chest. She sighed into him, relaxing. He leaned down to kiss her, and I wished I had done the same before we got home because she let him and even looked a little happy about it.

We ate together. The meal was delicious. For his tough man exterior, Rory could cook, and Lochlann wasn't half bad at it either. I watched as Ravena cleaned her plate and went back for more. Her face was thoughtful as she moved about the house, refilling our mugs and taking dirty plates away.

She stayed silent as she left us, walking down the hall to clean up. The smell of fresh water and floral soap wafted out from under the closed door. The soap smelled good but not nearly as good as she did on her own. The water ran for a long time, which meant she was thinking. I was learning her ways little by little, and that was one of them.

Rory walked outside to stoke the fire that heated the water for the house, and Lochlann went to the chaise and grabbed a book. I pushed my chair back from the table and sipped my ale. The house settled into a comfortable silence.

Ravena padded down the hall, her long, wet hair dripping down the back of her white shift. Tiny nipples peaked under the white fabric, and just the barest hint of pink showed through where her hair made it wet. Muscled, bare legs moved with such grace that my breath caught in my throat. I had never seen anything more lovely.

She paused, catching my stare. Need flashed through her eyes, making them so dark blue they looked like a midnight sky. Her fingers twitched as she walked past me, heading to the garden where Rory worked. The hint of desperation was hidden from her glance the moment I noticed it.

She opened the doors to the garden, closing them behind her without making a sound.

Lochlann and I looked at each other for the space of many heartbeats before looking away. We didn't get up to check on our mate- or our brother.

I've spent many a night wondering which of my brothers was the most damaged by Rowan, who is the darkest. Most nights, I would give that onerous distinction to Lochlann, but after Elic, Rory never recovered.

Neither one of them wanted the darkness that surrounds them, but it was there nevertheless. Lochlann can't sleep in the dark, and Rory wakes up screaming most nights. We all do, if I am honest. A piece is missing from all our souls, a piece that Rowan stole from us as children and continued to erode as we grew.

I looked through the door into the darkness of the night and hoped that perhaps Ravena could fix us all.

## Chapter Fourteen

### Rory

Like a wraith, she slipped through the garden and around to the shed where I hid. She was a goddess, and with her black hair and clear, blue eyes that soaked up the darkness, she looked ethereal. Her almost blue skin reflected what little light the moon shed, causing it to turn a deeper shade. I could just see the silhouette of her body through the thin fabric of her nightdress. I wasn't sure how I felt about it.

"You talked to Elic, didn't you?" I asked her, not meeting her eyes from where I sat hiding on a pile of wood.

"No. Elic didn't talk much," she said, moving into the small space of the shed.

"He usually doesn't shut up." I didn't mean my laugh to sound bitter, but it did anyway.

"Rory. I would never ask you to touch me if I'm not your type. I need to know, though, so that there are no misunderstandings. I want this to work. I need to know the rules." She leaned against the wall, her hands behind her back. Hard nipples poked through her gown as the night had turned chilly. At least I assumed it was the cool air that caused that particular reaction from her.

"You talked to Finn. Or Lochlann," I said, raising my eyes to hers. Her brows were clenched in worry, but there was no hint of contempt in her eyes.

"Finn told me, Rory, I'm only sorry it wasn't you. I know your life has been awful. It helps if I know what's going on, so I don't make it worse." She tilted her chin down, causing her hair to drape across her shoulder. "You know, we've never had sex. I can't lie, not all of the details of what has happened between the four of us are clear, but I know for sure that we have not."

"Rowan forced you to suck my cock one night while he took me," I said, my voice breaking in mid sentence, and I hated myself for it.

"Maybe so, that memory is distant and fading. Rowan was a horrible man; he was so far beyond redemption. Everything he did was awful, but you survived, and he did not," she said, her voice low but fierce. "We can make new memories to distance the old."

"We can. I've never been with a woman, Ravena. Lochlann and Finn assume I have been with you, but I have not. I don't know if I can. I've only ever been with men."

"If you don't want to be with me, you don't have to. I would never ask you to do that. It would be unfair and just as bad as anything Rowan ever did unless that is what you want. I was thinking, though, that if the Queen pushes the issue of a fourth man, maybe you could ask for Elic. It would allow you to be together under the guise of your union with me. You would be safer from her that way."

"Elic would never be your mate, Ravena."

She laughed, tilting her head back in delight. "Oh, I know that. I've seen elderly school mistresses more interested in those of the female persuasion than he is. Some of the loveliest females in the land came to the nursery today, and he had eyes only for their mates."

"You would bring him into your home for me. Knowing that he would never be yours, and I might not be either," I asked, sitting up a bit straighter.

"Of course, Rory. I don't want to leave. I don't want to be taken elsewhere. I have a chance at some brand of happiness here. We all do. In time, we should take it. Staying together protects us all. If he is what you want, then why should you not also find happiness?" Pushing off the wall, she came and perched next to me.

"What about love?" I asked.

"What about it?"

"Do you want it?" I turned to look at her. The soft smell of snow and falling rain mixed with her shampoo's floral scent relaxed something deep inside of me.

"Love is a dream we all hope to experience. Just because we started under difficult circumstances doesn't mean we all can't find it someday. Maybe together and maybe not. I hope together. Surviving shared trauma makes bonds. I care for all of you. I believe you care for me in some capacity as well. That's an excellent place to start. Only the Queen can break our contract and remove me from you. Barring that happening, we have a long time to figure the rest of it out." She leaned in and kissed my cheek before rising and walking away.

I sat in stunned silence, staring out into the darkness. Something in Ravena stirred me. Whether it was her sex or her kindness, I didn't know. Kindness was as foreign a concept as a female. I knew nothing of either. She didn't deserve a mate that didn't desire her, and I didn't deserve her comfort and affection.

Sighing, I rose, moving to follow behind her.

"I'm conflicted, Ravena," I said, stopping her forward progression. She turned and looked at me. Her eyes holding patience.

"Rory. There is no conflict. I will ask for nothing but your friendship if that is what you desire. We will be whatever you wish us to be." She placed her hand on my cheek, and I closed my eyes, leaning into it.

I didn't know what I wanted. Like Ravena, I've had little choice in my life. I inhaled her scent again, took her hand, and together we walked inside where the others pretended not to be waiting like nervous hens when their chicks wander too far.

Ravena looked lost for a minute, like she was unsure of what she should do next. She dropped my hand and went to the kitchen for a glass of water. She stood with her eyes closed and head tilted back just a bit, gathering her thoughts. Her long hair dusted the hem of the shirt and was the most beautiful thing I had ever seen. I would have done anything to take the look of worry off her face, but I couldn't do the one thing that might work. Not yet. Maybe not ever.

My insides were a twisted mess of history and pain, and my freedom was too new to trust. I hoped in time, the knots would ease. Until then, I would keep the shards of my broken soul to myself and cut no one else with them.

# Chapter Fifteen

## Ravena

Well, that didn't go exactly as expected, I thought as I fought to school my face into something, anything, other than what I was feeling inside. I felt like something was brewing. Like the hammer of some ancient God hung over our heads, ready to swing. Taking a deep breath, I sat the glass down and opened my eyes, trying to keep the uncertainty from shining through them.

Finn moved to me and brushed my hair back from my shoulder. He gave me a soft smile, and I returned it, although it did not reach my eyes.

"I feel a nightmare coming on; I don't suppose you could lay with me until I went to sleep?" The look in his eyes was not at all nightmarish and more bent to mischief.

"Is that so?" I asked, chuckling a little. I felt my smile widen, and my eyes fall into it.

"Yes. It's going to be a doozy of one too. A real humdinger." He waggled his eyebrows at me and grabbed my hand, leading me down the hall. His step light and the look in his eyes hopeful.

It was the most aggressive move any of them had made since I arrived, and I thought it cute. Having held Finn through more than a few nightmares, I knew that maybe he was sincere about that part, but that glint of something else made me tighten up in anticipation. I was going to say he started it, even if he didn't.

One torch was lit in the corner of his room and cast a soft glow across the space. A window out into the side of the garden let the moon shine through. He pulled his shirt off and eased onto his bed in only his soft sleeping shorts. Taking a deep breath, I tugged my shift over my head and dropped it on the floor.

I was not wholly sure about Finn. Honestly, I wasn't sure about any of them, but Finn was soft and sweet. Almost feminine. If I had to pick a brother not to be interested in women, it would have been him. In my time in the house, he had been the most abused by Rowan, yet somehow he stayed hopeful, and the darkness did not touch him.

His beautiful spirit shined from his eyes unbroken. Not like Rory. Not like Lochlann. He was the youngest, though, and maybe had fewer years during which to be broken.

Rowan's treatment of them all had been devastating. Still, Finn's almost feminine features seemed to have stirred something in him that caused extreme violence.

His quick intake of breath pulled my eyes to his face, and I watched him touch me everywhere with them. We had left the door open as no fire burned in his room to warm it. Maybe he hadn't thought I would come to him like this, but as he seemed not to mind, I slipped into the bed next to him.

He lay still as I traced the lines of his chest with my fingers. He was not muscled, not like the other two. He wasn't soft either; he just didn't share their definition. I traced the silky black trail of hair from his belly button down, stopping just shy of his cock before I ran my finger up his chest again.

His pants twitched, giving his secret away.

"Do you want me just to hold you, Finn?" His lips had parted, and his eyes darkened. "It's your choice."

"What is your choice?" he asked, threading his fingers through my hair. "I will take whatever you give, Ravena. Always."

I leaned down and kissed his lips, it started softly enough, but the fire spread as fires do. Given fuel, they become all-consuming.

My heart pounded as I slipped my tongue into his mouth, his chest rose against mine, and he deepened the kiss, bringing his hand behind my head to pull me to him. I snaked my leg over his hips and pulled myself on top of him. He stilled for a heartbeat.

"Is this too much? Do you want me to move?' I asked, pulling away to see his face.

"No. It's. It's new. It's nice. I'm okay. Remember, my magic makes unbreakable glass. I'm fine."

"You're more than fine; you are exquisite." I took his lips hard then, grinding myself against his erection. I let my appreciation of his beauty show on my face. Shaggy bangs covered part of his eyes, and I swept them away so I could see his face.

His hands came up to my hips, gripping them to him. I leaned up and cupped my breast, leading it to his lips. The groan that came from him shook his whole body, and I shivered when his tongue flicked my hardened nipple.

Need exploded out of me, and as much as I wanted to be slow and gentle with him, I wanted to take him hard. Maybe this is why Rowan couldn't restrain himself with Finn. Somewhere in Finn's magic was an attraction so deep it stirred arousal and need.

I eased back, forcing myself to slow. I calmed as Finn explored my breasts with his lips, teeth, and tongue. Wetness pooled between us, and I wanted to guide him into me but did not. He kissed up my neck and bit down on my earlobe, bringing a gasp from me. His lips found mine again; we kissed, softer this time.

Reaching down between us, he stood his cock up so that I could ease down on it. Just like with Lochlann, the feeling of him was so deep inside me as to almost hurt. I felt his tip push against the opening to my womb and cried out again, unable to stop myself. He reached deeper than Lochlann, and the feeling of him inside of me was exquisitely painful.

The grip on my hips eased, and he waited. Need rose from him so strong that I could smell it, but he did not move. Rising above him, I slid myself up his cock and lowered back down. He filled me so completely it took my breath, and I couldn't pull my eyes from his. I rose again, then found a rhythm in my movements and lost myself to it, raising and grinding until I threw my head back and came hard, clenching around him. His hands ran down my body and flicked my core, drawing a cry from me that turned the orgasm into something more.

My legs shook, and I couldn't keep up the effort. My head fell forward, and my black hair rested on his taut belly. He flipped me with little effort, pushing in deep and bringing another cry.

His lips met mine, our eyes still locked, and he drove in and out of me with intense precision. Angling his hips, he hit that spot they taught us about, and my cries turned to animalistic grunts. I came again, locking his flesh to mine. He pushed through and lost his precision, filling me so that it spilled out and soaked the sheets beneath us.

His kiss turned tender, and his hands light. He pulled me to him, covering us both. One of the others came in and extinguished the torch while we slept. I did not dream, and he had no nightmares.

But Rory Did.

His yells echoed down the hallway, and I was up and to him before I could think to grab my shift. I slid into his bed and pulled his back to me. He relaxed immediately, and a soft whimper escaped him. Wrapping my arms around him, I tucked his head under my chin and rocked him side to side until his ragged breaths slowed.

Finn came after and settled behind me, and together we soothed the nightmares into something else, and Rory slept. He slid the hair from my neck and kissed a line down the curve of it, then wrapped his brother and me in his arms. We slept that way until we heard Lochlann up and about.

Finn awoke first, and I felt him stir, sliding out of bed after sniffing my hair. He pulled it deep into his lungs, letting it out. He rose quietly, and I followed, letting Rory sleep longer.

"You are incredible," Finn said, brushing his lips across my forehead.

"I didn't do anything, Finn." I stood naked in the hallway as dawn's light spread across the sky.

"You care for us- for all of us. No one has ever done that. You take care of us. Our darkness doesn't scare you off."

I ruffled his long bangs out of his eyes. "There is no darkness here. Not anymore. Eventually, the light will win." I feinted left then dove right, stealing the washroom from him, shutting the door behind me. I heard him chuckle and walk away.

As they had to work, I bathed quickly so they could have their turn, dressing in a pale yellow dress that hugged my ribs then dropped to the floor. I went to my room and braided my hair in a complicated design before swiping some kohl around my eyes and a red stain on my lips. I went a little heavier today as they had said nothing about it yesterday.

I enjoyed wearing paints, stains, and dyes. Before I came to this house, I was an expert at applying them and often made up the other girls in secrecy. I hadn't been allowed to wear it after coming here. I had worn it that first day. When I was dropped at their door by the Queen's concierge, the first thing Rowan did after the other man left was to drag me to the bathroom and forcefully wash my face.

Then he slapped me hard enough to leave a mark and said never to decorate my face again without his permission. After, he yanked my new dress up over my hips, shoved me over the vanity in the washroom, and took my virginity from behind, grunting and sweating like a common pig as a thin trail of blood trickled down my legs.

I knew then what I was in for and just how awful this placement would be. Finn, Lochlann, and Rory watched in horror. Stunned to inaction and maybe a little relieved that perhaps some of the pressure would be off of them. I don't hold a grudge about that. Not one.

My torment lasted mere weeks; theirs had lasted a lifetime.


The other men went in and out of the washroom as I readied myself for a day filled with nothing. I had worked yesterday and would not go today. I planned to sit with Ari and perhaps visit the other girls or Finn's shop. There was nothing of him in this house save for a tiny glass bird he hung in my room, and I wanted to find something larger he had made to hang in the windows or on the walls. I would straighten our home and perhaps make dinner. I wasn't the best cook, but the brothers seemed to like it well enough, and they filled their plates every time I made something for them.

Quiet voices drifted from the kitchen as I twisted the last piece of the braid, securing it with a ribbon. When I walked down the hall and into the kitchen, all conversation ceased.

"Goddess, but you are beautiful." Lochlann walked to me, taking my hand.

"Thank you, Lochlann." I gave him a genuine smile. He wore his infantry uniform and looked dashing in it. Grey cloth and burgundy piping highlighted the beauty of his black hair and blue eyes. It took my breath. They were beautiful men. More beautiful every day.

"You look like artwork," Finn said, his hand drifting down from where it was. He wore light linen pants and a sky blue shirt that opened at his chest. His long bangs covered one eye, and he tossed his head to swing them back.

"You're a vision in yellow," started Rory. "Thank you for last night," he finished.

I went to kiss his cheek, patting his shoulder. "Let's hope that they ease with time."

He watched me, saying nothing; his eyes were cautious. He wore the moleskin hunting pants and a tucked-in burgundy shirt of the archers. His eyes deep blue like the magic lake on the far side of the realm. His pale skin marred here and there with scars from his many fights, and his nose sat just a shade crooked on his face. Few Fae had scars as we healed well, and most of our scars faded with time.

Rory's scars were pounded into him by the fists of many men. He was a fighter. They would never fade, but they did not detract from his beauty. If anything, they added to it.

Overcome with emotion, I turned from them. "I'll be at the bakery today. Ari and I have plans. She will bake things, and I am will eat them. I'll make dinner, though, so no worries there. I turned back to them when I thought I heard a groan.

"Dinner would be great!" Finn said, his eyes a little too wide. "We look forward to it."

Narrowing my eyes at him, I turned and left, closing the door behind me.

Once I was settled at the bakery with a muffin and some tea, I saw Lochlann and Rory call horses to them and ride away.

When I first came to the house, they walked to the Queen's stables and used the horses there. Over the last week or so, they had tried whistling for horses as some Fae do. After a day or two, they came. Short, fat little beasts showed up in pairs when they whistled now, and it made the brothers happy.

Finn worked so near that he had no need of a horse, but Rory and Lochlann often traveled far for their duties, and they seemed to enjoy their new horses and the freedom they gave them.

Myself? I did not like them. They are great hairy things with minds of their own and four feet to enforce their wills. I was happy to walk. I would never tell Ari my thoughts on this, for she would judge me harshly, and I did not need that. I watched with a soft smile as they rode away, feeling Ari's eyes bore into me.

"That's an interesting smile," she said. "Makes me wonder how things are going, sister." She laughed, and I turned my smile to her.

"Better. Much, much better." I smiled back, and I meant every bit of it.

## Chapter Sixteen

## Lochlann

Trouble was brewing, and I could smell it. We met at the training grounds and discussed recent events among ourselves. Last week there had been a melee of goblins causing trouble on the border, and now there was concern for Trolls. Orcs had been spotted near the capital, and the lesser Fae were antsy.

Dire wolf tracks came closer and closer to the city center, and there was a report of unicorns raging in the South. No one needs that; let me tell you. Those bastards are vicious.

Saige had warned Rory that he expected deployment to the border soon. No one was happy about it. We were all just getting settled after, well, everything. Now was not the time to leave. We all knew it.

We sparred with shields and spears, taking nothing seriously. I wanted nothing more than to go home for lunch, but the Captains' eyes were on us, and their unease kept us sparring.

When it was time to go, I rounded up Rory, who rounded up Finn, pulling him from the most beautiful creation I had seen him make. A flat pane of clear glass swirled with black, blue, and yellow. It reminded me of Ravena in her dress this morning. Beautifully complicated yet heartbreaking in its simplicity.

We walked home together as the spring sun settled behind the horizon. We stopped at Ari's bakery and grabbed a basket of bread and muffins as we had all heard Ravena's threat to make dinner. She is kind. She is a beauty. She is many things.

She is no cook.

We walked through the door to find some sort of crispy black meat on the table dressed with potatoes that looked a bit dry. Glasses of ale sat waiting, but there was no sign of Ravena. I called for her, and she didn't answer.

We found her outside, surrounded by greenery and blooming flowers. She had picked vegetables that would not be ready in other gardens for many weeks; they sat in a basket next to the lounge upon which she slept. Spring sun had pinked her nose and cheeks. Her yellow dress fanned out around her, and one arm lay flung over her head. We left her.

We stared down at the table in reluctance. She had worked so hard on this meal. It wasn't exactly her fault she couldn't cook. Maybe. There was a class on that, I am sure; perhaps she skipped those days.

Finn sawed a hunk of burnt meat and braved the potatoes. It took three glasses of ale each to get it down, but we did. When finished, we reached for cupcakes from the basket and sighed with pleasure, and that is how she found us.

She floated through the door, her messy black hair hanging in tangles around her shoulders. She smiled when she saw our empty plates and satisfied smiles. She was beautiful.

"I'm getting good at this," she said, her face alight with pleasure.

Rory choked on his dessert.

"You are getting very good at this, little bird. Thank you for dinner," I said, holding back a yelp when one of my brothers kicked me under the table, but it was no lie as I cannot tell one. She is getting better at everything. She works so hard to smooth our nerves and erase our scars. A lousy meal or twenty can't take away from that.

She grabbed one of the cookies from the basket and wolfed it down. Rory stoked the hearth fires as the chill was already creeping in. Finn was cleaning up the dishes, and Ravena had moved to change out of her dress. It was comfortable and domestic. Something I never thought I would experience.

I was just thinking about the perfection of the night when hooves clattered down the main road, skidding to a stop in front of our home. I went to the door to intercept whoever it was.

Loud banging on the door made Ravena jump. Rory pulled her behind him, shielding her. I'm sure he thought what I thought, that the Queen had come for her. Her light blue eyes were wide and terrified.

"Message from the Queen and orders from your Captains!" The Queen's page stood in full livery at our door. Two letters in his hands bore the Queen's seal.

I took the letters, and he sprinted to his horse and clattered away. Closing the door, I leaned against it breathing a heavy sigh.

"No," Rory said. "Not now." We shared a look between us. It was too soon. Our position with Ravena too tenuous.

It was a bad time to be separated. We had known it might come. Saige and Lann had both warned us something like this was coming; only they had darker imaginings than I did.

I knew they hated the Queen. Something had happened with Ari to make them hate her more. They spoke quietly of conspiracies and war.

Rory walked to me and took his letter, ripping it open and reading it.

"We've been summoned. Deployment is tomorrow with no end date. We must go to the southernmost border. We report to the palace in the morning at sunrise."

"What? Tomorrow?" Ravena's hand flew to her mouth, and her eyes grew even wider.

"Finn will be here, Ravena. It will be fine. Surely this is just a quick trip and nothing more. Like the Goblins we did a few weeks ago, it will be over in a day." I went to her and pulled her to me.

Finn stood back, looking worried, and Rory's face was darker than I had ever seen it. "Finn can close the shop, and you can stay close to the house until we return."

"No. Don't be ridiculous. I'm being silly, that's all. Finn has orders to fill, and I have the nursery. Everything is fine; I'm just dramatic." She stepped back and smiled into my face and relaxed in my arms.

"He's right, Ravena, you should stay close to home or over with Ari. No one is better with a sword. Not even Lann, though he claims he is, Saige says otherwise."

"I appreciate your concern, but it will be fine. Let's enjoy our last night together and get you packed up for tomorrow," she said, pulling us to her in a quick hug.

It didn't feel right. A deep sense of foreboding hung in the air as we moved about the house, readying to leave. Ravena folded clothes for packs, and Rory brought in more meat and vegetables from our storage outside. There was enough wood cut to see us through the spring, but other supplies like flour and sugar were getting low. Finn assured us that they would manage.

Ravena packed salted meat in containers and filled canteens with water and ale. I didn't have the heart to tell her that the crown would provide for us while we were gone. As she moved around the house, her brows grew closer together, and her scowl deeper. She said nothing.

Finally, when we were as ready as we could be, she slipped off down the hall. We heard water running as she bathed.

"Finn, take no chances. I have a bad feeling," I said when I was sure she couldn't hear.

"I won't. We'll keep our heads down." The concerned look on his face mirrored mine.

"Brother, take care of our girl," Rory whispered, reaching out and grasping Finn's forearm with his own. A quick look of surprise crossed Finn's face.

Neither of us believed that Rory would accept Ravena as anything more than a friend. I've never seen him talk with a female, not that we've had many opportunities, but there have been some. I always assumed he was only attracted to males. The look on his face made me wonder.

"Rory," I started. "Brother?" I asked.

"Don't," he said, walking down the hall and shutting his door.

I leaned back against the wall and sighed, getting ready to go change clothes myself. Rory would have to figure out Rory. None of the rest of us could.

Soft footsteps came down the hall, and Ravena stood, unsure. A thin white shift ghosted to her knees, and she had brushed the tangles from her hair. It hung dry and slightly curved at the ends. She had washed the face paint off and looked ready for bed.

"I," she started. "I don't know what to do," she finished, holding her hands together. She leaned against the opposite wall. I had never seen her look unsure, but at that moment, she looked at a total loss.

"What do you mean? There's nothing to do. We should get some sleep; dawn comes early." Pushing off the wall, I went to her. "You and Finn will be fine."

"I'm not worried about myself and Finn. I'm worried about you and Rory. Where you're going will be dangerous. I'm afraid for you." She looked up at me; her eyes were round and impossibly blue.

"We'll be safe. We have amazing fighters, and the archers are second to none. Even Rory isn't too bad," I said, earning a small smile from her.

"Okay. Well. Can I…can we stay together tonight? All of us? Just sleep?" Her voice trembled at the end, and just a hint of fear shone in her eyes.

No good had ever come to Ravena being with more than one of us at a time, and the good we had shared was new and fragile. That she suggested it at all was a surprise.

"Ravena," I stopped. "The only bed large enough to possibly hold all of us is Rory's."

Rory's bed that had been Rowan's.

"Will he mind?" she asked,

"Will you?"

"I've slept there. It no longer bothers me. I've stayed with Rory to help with his nightmares. You know that." I did know that. How she managed is the part I didn't understand.

"It's a great idea. It is. As long as Rory doesn't mind, I will ask him." I kissed her forehead and walked the hall to Rory's room to see if he would help soothe the fears of our little bird.

## Chapter Seventeen

### Ravena

I waited by the wall, indecisive about everything. The Queen's summons had thrown me for a loop, and I was nervous. Not for myself, not really, but for the men.

Something didn't sit right with me about the whole thing. I couldn't remember the last time the entirety of the Queen's regiments were summoned to any one place. Granted, I am not particularly old, but I feel the tension coming off of the men, too, despite their best efforts to hide it.

I wanted to be with them all, to sit and talk all night, but I understood that they needed rest, and tonight could be their last night of decent sleep. I was nervous too. Maybe a little afraid. I was feeling many things I couldn't nail down. I followed Lochlann down the hall.

His bulky frame blocked my view of Rory; their words were short, tense, and stopped when I came to a halt behind him.

"It's okay, Lochlann. I understand. You should all be comfortable tonight. Sleep well." Overwhelmed and exhausted, I turned and padded down the hallway to my room.

"Wait. Ravena," Rory said. "I want you to stay. I do." His voice was soft, emotion clogging his throat.

I stopped, not turning, not going forward.

"Please," he finished.

I turned and walked back. Lochlann moved aside and let me pass. I went to the bed and slid under the covers next to Rory, keeping my body from touching his. Lochlann moved into me from behind and adjusted his large frame until he was wrapped lightly around me.

Finn came out of the washroom, his long, black bangs dripping over his face. He walked past Rory's door, stopped, and backed up.

"Um?" he asked, one eyebrow arched.

"Pile on Finn. Ravena wants us to keep her company tonight." Rory laughed for the first time, and it was real, musical, and so good to hear.

"Incoming!" Finn took three steps and jumped into the middle of us, causing everyone to screech, laugh, and shuffle.

Finn settled on the other side of Rory, and we snuggled, stretched, and wormed our way into comfortable positions. None of us had lit a torch, and the room was dark and silent as we drifted off to sleep. Someone's hand was on my hip, and another hand reached into my hair.

There were no nightmares, and sleep came over us like rain, slow at first, then heavy and thunderous.

I awoke under muscled arms with a hairy leg draped over me. My face was buried in Rory's armpit, which was soaked from my drool. His arm wrapped around my head and cradled it to him.

Pulling my limbs to me, I set off a cascade of flesh as they shifted and parted, allowing me to get up. I felt lighter than I had the night before and more hopeful than I had in a while. A good night's sleep will do that for you.

I put on tea in the kitchen and scrambled some eggs for the men, charring the edges a little and hurrying to fold those sections in so they wouldn't be noticeable. I buttered bread and threw some kind of sausage in with the eggs to cook, proud of my creativity.

They would love it.

Taking off my apron, I took a torch and walked into Rory's room, lighting his. The ghost of Rowan did not assault me. It was just a room. A place where once upon a time abhorrent things happened, but now good ones had taken their place.

"Boys," I said, shaking a random foot. "The sky is lightening; I made breakfast." Groans rose from the pile of men, and I smiled. They looked like little boys all snuggled together, not wanting to get up. I didn't want them to get up either. I hoped one day to see a pile of their sons act just like this.

The thought stilled my heart, and I almost fainted. I am so not a fainter, but Gods, how could I even consider having children? Not as long as Aramea was Queen. Should I have a pile of sons, she would kill them. I couldn't do that to them, myself, the men, or anyone. There could be no children.

I left them to get up and get dressed alone, going into the kitchen to pile heaps of food onto their plates and pour them some tea.

"Oh. Ravena. You shouldn't have gone to the trouble," Lochlann said, coming up behind me with a quick hug and a kiss on my head.

"It was no trouble." I watched as they gave one another dark looks. I knew they didn't want to leave. It was showing. In fact, they took just a few bites and pushed their plates away.

"I can't eat, love," Finn said, grabbing my hand from across the table. I'm too nervous about today.

"Me either!" Rory almost shouted. "I mean, me too. My stomach is in knots."

"It's understandable," I said, scraping their untouched breakfast into my compost pile. It would make excellent fertilizer.

We walked out together, Lochlann and Rory, with their packs slung over their big shoulders. My stomach began to quiver too. I did not want them to go. I'm not sure why. I didn't love them, but I cared. They were my friends, and we had fun together. What little sex we had post Rowan was satisfying, and I wanted more time to explore that.

More than anything, I felt safe with them. For the first time since leaving my sisters, a sense of belonging and safety had buffeted me from the violence that is Talamh na Sithe. Not that Finn wouldn't protect me, he would, but the edge of unease settled into my soul like a sharp knife.

Watching them walk toward the armory outside of the castle, I worried our time together may have run out.

So many were there saying goodbye to their mates, brothers, lovers, and friends. All of The Eight were there, and that gave me pause. I saw Ari hugging her men hard and long. Our eyes met, and the look she gave me was filled with worry and anger. She loved them already, and I was a little jealous of that for some reason. They kissed her and held her like they might never see her again, and my worry turned to fear. If Ari was worried, there might be more cause for concern than I understood.

The feeling of bad tidings grew deeper. Ari gave me a grim nod and returned her focus to the four gorgeous men surrounding her, vying for her attention. She was losing three mates to the Queen's border and did not look happy about it.

As I looked around, I noticed that many of my sisters said goodbye to two men. Only Ari and I were left with one mate at home. Talamh na Sithe is far too dangerous for one man to keep one woman safe. We would have to stay together, all of us, to take some of the burden off of the ones left behind.

I hugged Lochlann to me and brushed my lips across his. He grabbed me hard and kissed me back, slipping his tongue between my lips. I sank into him and gave him the kiss he wanted. When he pulled away, I hugged Rory, placing a chaste kiss on his cheek. He held me to him, sniffed my hair, then let me go.

Finn grasped their forearms and pulled them into tight, long hugs. The herald blew his horn, and the men gathered into companies and rode away. A collective shudder went through those left behind.

"I'll stay with you today, or you can come to the shop if you want and help me with a project for the house," Finn said, placing his hand on my elbow.

"I have no intention of getting in your way, Finn. Walk with me to the nursery, and I'll see to the plants, then go stuff myself on the cakes I'm sure Ari will be baking." I threaded my arm through his, allowing him to lead me away from the square.

The soft blue dress I chose this morning shushed through my legs, brushing his pants. The town was quiet; a subdued stillness hung in the air. The walk was not a short one, and some of my tension eased before we got to the huge, glass building where I would work my magic.

If I chose, I could touch them all from the door and go home, but the smell of damp soil and freshwater calmed me. I would enjoy touching each plant and tailoring my magic to its needs.

Finn kissed my cheek, "I'm just down the road if you need me."

"Thank you; I'll be fine. I'll see you at home. I'll grab something from the diner."

"Don't go in there after dark, love. Wait for me if it gets late, and we'll go together." He was worried, too; I could see that. He couldn't hide anything in those deep blue eyes. They were like a crystal clear lake; you could see straight to the bottom of them.

"I'll be careful." I gave him a smile that tried hard to reach my eyes before turning into the nursery to lose myself in the greenery.

I worked for several hours, touching each plant, watering them, pulling stray weeds, and moving around displays. There wasn't a plant that did not flourish. Even the plants that had been near death upon my last visit had perked up and thrived. It was my magic.

Magic is a weird thing, and I've never understood it. One would think all Fae would have similar talents and skills, but we do not. Ari can do anything, but she is the exception. Her magic is in her cakes as mine in my plants, but she can also shoot fireballs and make potions that heal. She can take a plant

I grow and make it do anything she wishes, and her garden grows as well as mine.

We know the land is dying, and we all know why. History says our magic has weakened. I wonder what I could do if it had not? What could we all do? If I could shoot fireballs, I would not have had to ask my sister to end Rowan for me.

The men have very little magic. Rory's arrows flew straight and hit their mark every time. He has healing magic for minor things but nothing more. Finn's ability with glass is beautiful, but I don't know that he has any other magic. Lochlann? I had never seen him perform any magic at all and thought maybe he had none.

I was deep in thought when Elic approached me. "You're very far away today, Ravena," he said. His silver hair was brushed back from his face and secured in a knot at the back of his head. He came to my chin, and I had to look down to answer.

"I suppose I am." I turned from the plant my hand had stilled over, offering him a small smile.

"Rory told me what you said. About me staying with you and the brothers. Did you mean it?" he asked, his face a blank page.

"I did. If Rory wants that and it will make him happy, then yes, Elic. None of us asked for this if that makes sense." I smoothed my hands over my dress, making little dirt trails as usual. My clothes were never clean.

"It does. And thank you. It means a lot. For what it's worth, I don't think Rory cares for only me." He smiled back, and I thought, just maybe Elic and I could become friends. Maybe even good friends. "I think your magic touches more than just plants, Ravena." He bumped my shoulder with his and smiled.

"I'm going to Ari's for tea and muffins. Would you like to come?" I asked, feeling much better walking out of the nursery than I had walking in.

"I would love to," he said, drawing the word 'love' out. "Besides, we can't have one of Faerie's most beautiful women walking around alone.

"Goddess, not you too." I laughed, and together, we walked to Ari's.

He sat for a bit, joking and laughing with the other girls that had gathered there by their accord. He preened and said that he was the only smart man in town since he was surrounded by more females than any one man ever had been.

The girls took him to heart and laughed along with him; he glowed from their attention and fit right in. As the morning went into afternoon and the other girls' mates came around for them, he filtered off too, saying he had work.

Ari and I were left alone. Not long after midday, the Queen came into the bakery. None of us liked her, but she terrified me.

At this moment in time, no, in every moment in time, she held the lives of The Eight in her hands. Only Ari had the strength to fight her, and she didn't often.

I tried not to let my fear show as she greeted us, calling us her favorite murderesses. If she were smart, she would understand that she, herself, was her favorite murderess. Ari and I may have killed one man, but the Queen had killed thousands.

I assured her that Rowan died a happy man and that it wasn't my fault he was weak. It was all I could do to keep my hands from shaking. The Queen watched us with the eyes of a snake. We were taught a story in history class about the Christian God and how a snake ruined his paradise's perfection. Aramea was that snake.

She taunted Ari and ate her pastries, but oddly Ari said nothing. My heart worried more, and I felt the breeze from the hammer swinging above our heads. Something was off in Talamh na Sithe if Ari did not lob at least one fireball at her mother. It made my heart still.

We were left in peace and spent the rest of the day in an uncertain limbo. It was as if the very air in Talamh na Sithe was deciding what move came next, and we were the pieces in the game awaiting direction. It was unsettling to the core, and we all felt it. Ari and I held hands and continuously spoke to fill the strained silence. It was not our best day.

## Chapter Eighteen

### Finn

I opened the door to Ari's bakery and found her and Ravena huddled at a table. Their faces pale and almost touching as they spoke. I looked around and saw no threat, but the air was heavy with it.

"What's the matter?" I asked, closing the door behind me and looking around.

"Nothing," Ari said. "The Queen was here. That's all." She gave a deep roll of her eyes and rose from the table to grab a basket.

I knew Ari hated her mother; everyone did. I brushed it off.

I hadn't been able to work much; I couldn't stop worrying about my brothers and thinking about Ravena. I made it as long as I could then came to find her.

"Your dinner is in here; stay close to your house if you can. Something isn't right; I can feel it," she said, handing me the heavy basket. The smell of spiced meat drifted from under the cloth covering it.

"That seems to be the consensus," I said. "Thanks for this." I hefted the basket; her smile was wide and genuine.

"I love you, sister, be safe," she said, hugging Ravena to her.

"I love you too, Ari. You be safe. Stay away from your mother." They clung together for a long moment.

"I will." Ari stepped back and waved goodbye.

Once inside, I barred the door to our home, something we rarely, if ever, do. We never felt we had to. I spread the food from the basket on the table. Ravena and I feasted on tender spiced meat, golden buttered potatoes, and garden beans. Together we cleaned up and went into the back garden to enjoy the last of the sunlight.

Ravena knelt, touching her plants and picking ready vegetables while I picked up errant sticks, tossing them into the firepit. The last rays of the sun captured the darkness of her hair, making it glitter. Her skin lit this way lost its blueish tint and looked like soft moonlight; the delicate curve of her cheek showed through the curtain of her hair. Goddess, she was beautiful.

My cock started to rise in my pants, and I took a chance. We had all been so careful of one another since Rowan died. None of us wanted to push. It's like we walked on eggshells. We worried so much about boundaries and fear. I went to her, sinking my hands in her hair as she bent down to touch some green thing.

I pulled her hair gently back, not wanting to scare her but needing her more at that moment than I ever had. She gazed back at me, surprise changing to something darker, and I saw a side of our delicate Fae I had not seen before. Desire darkened her eyes, and her pupils dilated to cover almost all of the blue at my not so gentle touch.

I dragged her to me, crushing her with my kiss. She responded beautifully, pressing her willowy body to mine. Our tongues clashed, and teeth scrapped in our rush to take each other. Her hands ran down my body, gripping my cock through my pants, causing me to take a sharp breath.

Through her dress, I cupped her breast, pinching her nipple, then pinching it harder when her moans deepened. Her head sank back, and I buried my face in her neck, biting up the side of it and gripping her earlobe with my teeth. She bucked against me, rubbing herself along my hardness.

Reaching around, I pulled the laces of her dress and slid it down her body until she stood in front of me naked. Glorious. She wore no bindings on her small breasts, and I slipped her underwear to her ankles as I slid down her body with my tongue, stopping to bury it in her sex.

She cried out, tugging at my hair. The sharp scent of her was all female, and my cock grew so hard it pained me. Bumping her legs apart, I dug into her with my tongue, pulling out to caress the swollen nub with it. She grabbed my shoulders harder and held on as her legs shook.

I took the backs of her thighs in my hands, pulling her onto my face. I loved the way she tasted, the way she smelled, and the way she went limp with my touch. I never wanted to be careful again. I wanted this. I needed it. She was mine, and I was hers. I flicked her core once, twice, and on the third flick, she came onto my face, drenching me with her pleasure.

I took two fingers and pushed them deep inside her, drawing out her orgasm. Her muscles clenched around them, and I groaned into her. Pulling another flurry of contractions and cries from her. Her legs began to shake, and she used me to support most of her weight.

I picked her up in my arms and carried her inside to her room. None of us had ever been with her there, not since it became hers. But I needed to have her there. I needed to have her in her space and prove that she would be safe with me anywhere.

I slid her onto the bed and spread her legs with my body, pushing into her in one stroke as I planted my face in her neck to inhale the sweet scent of her. Then I waited. I felt her breathe. Felt her relax around me. Pulling back, I took her mouth hard again, letting her taste herself on my tongue.

Everything about her was exquisite. The velvet feel of her on my cock, the sweet scent of her in my nose, and the taste of her in my mouth. I pushed into her again, and she arched against me, tilting her pelvis to pull me in deeper.

Need overtook sense, and I slid into her harder and harder, hitting her deep inside and feeling the firm barrier of her cervix on my cock's head. I pushed harder and angled beyond it. I watched her fall apart under me, under the push of my hips. Her face tightened, shattered, and remade itself into something different. Something calm, safe, and satisfied.

She clenched my cock, pulling my orgasm from me, and I bathed her with my seed, hoping for the first time that I might make her pregnant. Goddess, that moment. None compared. She rode me like a wild thing as the last bit of her orgasm made her shake, pulling more and more seed of my seed into her body until I was empty.

In the end, I collapsed on top of her, taking in her closed eyes and soft smile. I wouldn't apologize for being rough. I could see the happiness on her lips. Her body forced mine out, and a flood of fluids flowed from her, drenching both of us. I brushed the hair from her face as her breathing slowed.

Reaching for her, I kissed her lips, her cheeks, her face, and her smile grew wider. Her blue eyes popped open, taking me in. She had never looked more beautiful.

"Bathe with me?" She asked.

"I would love to," I answered, rising even though I wanted nothing more than to stay with her in her bed covered in our fluids.

I wrapped a towel around my hips and went to fill the outdoor water heater and light hearth fires while the tub filled. It was a large tub, made for large men, and would take a bit.

Ravena stood naked in the kitchen, licking the frosting from a cupcake off her fingers. I had never seen her so unguarded. Black hair drifted down her back and draped her ass in beauty. I walked past her, closing the doors behind me.

I saw a flash of gray clothing and pale hair through slats of the high fence surrounding the garden. Running footsteps echoed from the alleyway behind our house and Ari's bakery. I didn't think of giving chase. Instead, I stuck my head through the gate and made sure no one else was there. Cum dripped down the back of the fence onto the high grass. Closing the gate, I barred it too. Rushing through the rest of the chores, I hurried inside, checking every door and every window to be sure they were secure. My breath came in gasps as I rushed to find Ravena.

She lay in the tub, arms draped over the cold, white porcelain. She raised her head and gave me a smile that froze when she saw my face.

"Are you okay? Is something wrong?" she asked, sitting up. Her long hair covered her breasts, but her pink nipples peeked through it.

"Everything's fine. I was just in a hurry to get back to you," I said, forcing myself to relax. It wasn't a lie. Not really. Just an omission and the Fae can omit with the best of them.

Her smile relaxed, and her face opened. I stepped into the tub facing her. Her legs stretched across mine. Taking first one foot and then the other, I massaged her arches and up her calves. The water was just shy of too hot, but it felt amazing on my skin. I soaped her legs, leaning over her to reach her breasts and arms.

I let my fingers drift lower and massaged between her legs.

"I thought this was a bath," she laughed, her eyes closed and face slack.

"It is a very thorough bath, my lady," I said, pushing her hair aside and cupping her breasts with both my hands. I bit down on one, bringing the peak into my mouth. I pulled on it hard, taking it deep.

She gasped, "So it is, Sir." She opened her eyes and pinned me with them. She rose, pushing me back from her as she straddled my hips.

I took a cup and soaked her hair, massaging the fantastic floral shampoo she used into it before rinsing it out. She filled her hands with shampoo and did the same to me. My moan echoed through the small space of the room at the feel of her fingers on my scalp; I had felt nothing like it before.

She rolled her hips against my growing erection and washed down my chest, circling my nipples with soap and her fingers. Leaning into me, her breasts dancing across my chest, she took my mouth. Teasing and slow, she kissed me. Her hair drifted around us like a curtain, and my cock was filled and heavy again.

She ground against me, reaching between us, she positioned herself over me and sank down. I filled her slowly as she took her time, rising and sliding down again until she had taken me to the hilt. She watched my face as she rose above me, tilting her hips so that her core rubbed against my pelvis. She used me to bring herself, and I leaned back and watched.

She was passionate. Full of fire. We hadn't seen it, hadn't been allowed to see it. I hadn't seen it, but I saw it now. I saw her. She found her pleasure and allowed herself to enjoy it. She threw her head back as she came on my cock. Water sloshed around us, and she rode me hard. Her breasts bouncing against me. I let her take me how she wanted. I kept my hips firm but did not move them so she could use me to please herself. And she did. She came one more time before her head sank onto me, and she curled against my body.

Her soft lips found my neck, and she kissed me in the curve of it. She had emptied me so completely the first time that I thought about pulling out and letting my erection soften, but she rolled her hips once more and raised her eyes to mine in question, and I changed my mind.

I flipped her, pulling her hips out of the water, and entered her from behind. She cried out and rounded her back into me. I reached around and flicked her nub hard.

"I can't. I can't come again, Finn," she panted as she braced against the punishing pace of my thrusts.

"You will come," I ordered, thrilling at the sound of my command. "I will make you."

I thrust as I flicked until she did come. With a startled cry that tapered to an exhausted moan, she clenched around me again, then sagged against the side of the tub as I threw my head back, gripped her hips, and finished deep inside of her.

I rewashed her, rinsing our juices off. She lay limp in the tub, eyes closed and face slack. I scooped her out, wrapping her in a towel. I dried her off and placed her under her covers, sliding in to pull her close. She let out a long sigh that spoke of many things.

I would worry about the person outside our gates tomorrow. Tonight, there was only her. Only us. I settled my chin on top of her head, and together we slept.

# Chapter Nineteen

## Ravena

Holy Fuck, I could barely walk. There were no words for how amazing, incredible, fantastic, passionate, and sexy Finn had been last night. Wait, there were a lot of words, but none of them are enough. Great Goddess, *that* is what it's supposed to *be* like. I'm certain I heard birds singing and the Goddess laughing that last time. I'm also certain my heart stopped and restarted. I had died last night and woke up as something new. I was healed.

Finn let me grow, and I let myself trust him. The weeks since Rowan's death had paved the way to that moment. To last night. He showed a side of himself I had not seen. In those moments of passion, we learned about one another.

Finally. Honestly. I knew him. I could accept his gentle side or rough one and would revel in them. He had lit a fire, and Goddess knows it still burned, despite the soreness between my legs.

No longer was this an effort to make us safe and ease their fears. Oh no. Phase two involved sex. Lots and lots of sex. Even Rory, unless he told me no. If he only wanted men in truth, then I would let it go, but he had never had a woman, so until he had one and decided it wasn't for him, then I was giving myself the go-ahead.

I needed him. I needed all of them. We could take the broken parts of ourselves and meld them together into one complete whole. The euphoria of those orgasms made the path before me so clear. I waxed on its beauty and felt like a philosopher and a sex goddess rolled into one. That is the power of a good orgasm.

Finn and I had risen together, dressing and getting ready in the haze of domestic bliss. I missed Rory and Lochlann at that moment, and I knew he did too. We drank tea and ate muffins, our hands never leaving the other's body for long. A longing so deep within me bubbled up, and I wanted him again, but he seemed worried and maybe even a little distracted. He checked the doors and windows twice before we left, and I wondered if Ari's warnings had bothered him.

He walked me to Ari's and begged me to stay with her until he could come back for me. Something about his ferocity made me agree, and the promise settled over us. He relaxed and smiled.

"I won't be long," he said. "I have the piece for our home almost done, and two clients are picking up glass today, and then I will come back for you."

He took my hands in his and looked into my eyes, his eyes so sharp they could cut ice.

"Okay, staying with Ari is no hardship," I said, laughing.

Ari watched us with a knowing smile on her face that shined into her eyes and made her face look soft. One thing Ari has never been soft. She loves her men; perhaps love had changed her.

Finn walked away, leaving The Eight alone. All of us had congregated in Ari's bakery again, by some unspoken pull, we came and shared tales of men.

Teagan was having a time of it; she had already been moved once and thought she would be moved again. Arlie, Keena, Keelin, and Ari were all happy and gushing about great sex, twosomes, threesomes, and so on. Arlie was the freest of us all and talked at length about her life. She and Keelin wanted babies.

Did I want a baby? No. And I thought they were fools for wanting them. Ari gave out her contraceptive potion to those that wanted it and spread around the extra she had brought that the others did not want.

I don't think anyone believed that we would have children. Eight young women would not fix what many; many others had tried and failed to. The Goddess would give us children or not, and I believed she would not. Not until there was a change. Not until the land was healed.

I was okay with that, even if others were not.

We sat into the growing morning, talking unabashedly about everything. Even me. I shared that things had changed and that we were healing. My rosy face and happy laugh told them more than words could, and my friends smiled at me. These girls were my life, and I was theirs. Having a sister is like having a piece of yourself in another's body. We would always love each other.

It was deep into the morning when screams echoed through the streets, first one and then many. Ari grabbed her sword and barred the door, blocking us with her tiny body. The change was instant, and I knew I had been wrong. There is still nothing soft about her. Love had not made her weak. If anything, it made her more fierce.

Her red hair flowed around her as she released her magic, and her sword began to glow. She pushed us into her storeroom and hid us behind her counter despite our protests. She stood alone and faced the storm of green that flowed through the streets like a river.

We had all taken a swordsmanship class. Most had sweated and slaved for their C's and D's; I had failed mine miserably. Only Teagan had gotten a B minus, but Ari had lived and breathed it. Her skill with a sword is unparalleled. As Trolls bigger by half than our largest Faeman rushed through the streets, smashing and killing everything in their way raged, Ari stilled. A calm came over her like nothing I had ever seen before.

A Troll outside raised its head and sniffed deep into its nose. His eyes turned and locked on Ari. Her sword did not shake, and she did not hesitate. It crashed through the window, grabbing for her. She ducked and sliced, and it screamed as its arm came off.

With his other hand, he struck at her; she dove under its reach, rolled, landed on her feet, and struck it again, slicing into its legs and taking it down. But Trolls are a nasty thing. Large and hearty. They are challenging to kill, and Ari was overrun.

Trolls rolled through the broken glass, one over top the other. They flowed like a flash flood, and we were all caught up in them. Something grabbed my ankle, and I was thrown over a shoulder, Ari's sword and magic made the thing release me, and I was thrown through the glass, claws grabbing at me as I flew. Aileen landed in a broken heap next to me. Blood dripped fast and steady between her closed eyes. I stumbled with her to my house, shoving her in and closing the door.

I went back and pushed, pulled, and dragged any girl I could get my hands on. They were tossed by Ari or dropped by bloodied Trolls, and I took them, evading the grasping Trolls and the lobs of Ari's fireball magic. Arlie screamed, and I saw a Troll sprint with her. Ari lobbed fireballs, singeing the thing's back, and it bellowed from pain but did not drop Arlie. It was gone before any could stop it.

Ari fought like no creature I had ever seen before. Her dance was beautiful, deadly, and terrible to see. Slicing Trolls and lobbing magic at them until they were beaten back, she whirled, twisted, and slashed as her long red hair flowed behind her like barley in the wind. I grabbed Finley and dragged her to my house, returning in time to see Teagan in the grasp of a Troll and his bloodied back running as Ari scrabbled onto him like an animal, trying to force him to drop the girl.

The Troll threw Ari, and she landed in a heap. Blood covered every part of her, and she looked fierce as Trolls ringed her, suddenly ignoring the rest of us. She met my eyes over the Troll's shoulder and gave a sad, knowing smile. Turning, she sprinted away, and every remaining Troll followed.

I knew something then, knew it in my bones. Those things had been after her. Taking the others was a bonus, but they had come for her. Why were our men hunting Trolls on some distant border when they were in our town? Why indeed. I don't know much about Trolls, but this level of cooperation and teamwork seemed out of character for the beasts.

I crawled to my knees, blood ran down my arms, and I tasted it in my mouth; I watched as it dripped into the soil from where I rested on all fours, my head hung as I gathered strength. Parts of my face hurt, and I was having difficulty taking a deep breath, but I would live.

Laith came screaming, his sword drawn, and his face panicked.

"Ari?" he demanded.

"To the crossroads. Hurry. She fought so hard. She saved us." I collapsed onto the ground, tasting dirt, sobbing and hysterical. I couldn't lose her. I couldn't lose any of them, but especially not her.

Strong arms grabbed me up and rolled my bloodied and dirty body into theirs. I knew by the scent that it was Finn. He always smelled of thyme and cherries. His scent came to me, and my brain registered that I was safe.

"Finn, the girls. They need help. Put me down." I sniffed, getting my panic under control.

"I can't let you go. I can't let you go. I can't let you go." Finn rocked me, frantic. His arms trembled.

"You won't be letting me go, Finn. You'll be helping me help them. We have to help them," I said as the screams and cries pierced the air around me.

He nodded once and put me down, rushing to wipe his tears on his sleeves. I swayed on my feet, then straightened. His sharp intake of breath when he took me in let me know I was hurt. I could feel it. I pushed through the fear and pain and ran to the bakery.

Laith had said Keena was injured, and I found her slumped on a pallet in the storeroom. Her arms and legs were at odd angles, and her face ashen. Her chest rose and fell, but just barely. I knew Ari kept healing potions at her home, but I assumed she would have some stashed here as well.

I tore through drawers and ransacked shelves.

"Look for a small green bottle, Finn. There has to be one here somewhere," I said, not caring that I was sacking the place even more.

"This?" he asked, holding up a tall, green bottle that had been discarded in the attack.

"No, smaller than that. About half that size," I said, taking the tall bottle and shoving it into the pockets of my dress.

"What is that one for?" He turned from me, moving behind the counter.

"Not for healing. If you want to know, I will tell you, but now we need to find the other potion." I looked to where he knelt on the floor, rifling through things under the counter.

Distrust slid across his face and was gone; I would tell him. I would. They deserved to know; I just hoped they understood. These Trolls had made the point for me. No one was safe in the Capital. No one was safe in Talamh na Sithe. Ari was probably dead. Teagan and Arlie were taken and would follow Ari down that path. Why would I want an innocent baby to suffer in this place?

"Here," he said, handing me a small blue bag that was closed with a drawstring. I heard glass tinkling and hoped he was right.

Opening the bag, I dumped out a handful of short green bottles and one black, smokey one. My breath caught in my throat, and I hurried to stash the black bottle back in the bag.

"...Ravena." Finn looked at me, his eyes round and impossibly sad.

"Never for you, Finn. I swear. I swear on my life, never for you. Not you. Not Rory. And not Lochlann. It was my only recourse. Our only recourse. I am no murderess. I swear it," I begged him with my eyes to understand, even as I tucked the black bottle deep into the folds of my dress.

The Queen could never be allowed to find it.

"Take one of the healing potions, Ravena. Please," he added at my dark look. "You've been clawed down both arms, and your nose may be broken."

"Keena is much, much worse. I will heal. We will see if others need them; if there are any extra, I will take one." I took the short green bottle and forced it to Keena's lips, making her drink.

Her breathing settled, and her color improved.

"We must straighten her limbs if we can. I don't know if they'll heal crooked otherwise," I said, going around to where her legs lay, one almost backward.

Finn didn't argue. His face soured and took on a green cast as we pulled her limbs straight, ignoring her cries of pain. Donovan, one of her mates that remained at home, came running, shouting her name at the top of his lungs.

"Let her rest, Donovan. I gave her a healing potion," I placed my hand on his arms to stop him from picking her up.

"What happened? What the fuck happened?" he keened, dropping beside her. His eyes only for her.

I filled him in the best I could, then Finn and I went to see what we could do for the others.

Fae are hard to kill. Very hard. But not impossible. Dead Fae littered the streets, lying broken and discarded.

Trolls had ripped off heads and cut through spines. A true Healer could have fixed them. Maybe. But the land had not seen one of those in many hundreds of years, if not thousands. Ari's healing potion could not help them.

I gave the few bottles I had to the old Fae woman that owned the diner, Aron, Keena's other mate left in the capital, Max, Keelin's mate, and Zane, one of Arlie's men. They had rushed to the screams and been run through with swords in various places. I couldn't be sure that they would survive, but I was hopeful. Ari's healing potion was the best in the land.

The Queen did not come. Not then. As people fought to save their neighbors and loved ones, she was nowhere to be found. The screaming had faded to low moans long before we saw her face. Only later. After the funeral pyres were lit, she came, asking after her people, asking about Ari. There was something so contrived about it that the marrow of my bones chilled, and I saw her, really saw her.

The self-satisfied smile on her face did not go unnoticed when she was told her daughter was missing, and I was not the only one who noted it. The problem for the Queen lies in the fact that Talamh na Sithe loved Ari. She is a favorite daughter, and she should be. She is fierce and loyal. She is brave and honorable. She is all the things the Queen is not, and in those moments after the events of the day, the tide began to turn against her.

## Chapter Twenty

### Rory

The border was quiet. Too quiet. Once upon a time, I went to the furthest reaches of a place called Tir fo Thuinn. It is a stormy, oceanic place where the sky is always yellow with warning. That is was what the border reminded me of. Like there was a great storm on the horizon that caused the sky to yellow and the winds of change to blow.

The Queen's best trackers had found nothing. Seal, Ari's huntsman, had already told a select few that he was slipping home tonight. Every Faeman felt the unease, but none could put the finger on it.

Then she came. The white Wraith that was Ari's odd mare came screaming along the front lines, mad and striking at anything in her way. Great chunks of flesh were ripped from the thing's side, and the only thing keeping her from death was the will to live. She had tiny, bloody handprints on her ravaged sides. Every man to a one froze, and fear rippled across company lines, and we knew. We all knew.

That mare never left Ari's side. If Ari walked hand in hand with her mates in the park, that mare ghosted behind them, hugging the tree line. If Ari was in the bakery, the mare waited at the nearest shade tree. She was joined to Ari in an unusual way for a Fae horse, but no one really believed the mare to be a Fae mare.

She may not be of the Goddess, but she was of something else.

Seal, Lann, and Saige converged upon the mare, calming her. In a moment, the horns sounded, and we thundered as one back to the capital. Half a day's ride cut into a few hours. Many horses died on that trip, but no man stopped trying to reach the Capital.

It had to be bad, and we knew it. I had thought my life to be filled with old fears. Fear of rape. Fear of Rowan. Fear of death. Fear of life.

I had never known real fear before that moment.

Never.

Fear almost paralyzed me. Fear for Finn. Fear for Ravena. Whatever happened, she would have been with Ari, and the small bloody handprints on the side of the white mare had glowed like heart blood. Like the blood that pumps from a man until he dies if it is not stopped.

Fear. That is true fear.

I kicked my stallion and rode behind Ari's mates. We thundered across the land, and the sound of desperate hoof beats lulled me into a place where I could only think about fear.

I had no idea where Lochlann was; I did not look for him. He would be in this mass of men, but I had to get to her first. I had to get to her now.

I had never touched Ravena in kindness. I had only raped her mouth at my brother's command, trying not to notice as she gagged and coughed around me when Rowan slammed her head over my cock again and again as tears ran down her face.

Still, she held me in the dead of night when my dreams took me back to a time when my small, childish body was stretched around his, meaty hands held my throat, threatening, always threatening as he tore me from the inside out.

She had held me, and I forgot to be afraid of the dark. Forgot to be afraid of nightmares. All I had ever done was force myself on her in the way that had been done to me. I was more afraid of Rowan than of breaking an innocent woman. I had never kissed her lips. Not once.

Did I desire women? How could I know? All I had done was hurt the one I had access to, and still, she held me when I screamed.

She had taken my brothers and was remaking them. I knew what she was doing; she had no choice, had never had a choice. We were the same, she and I. She made Finn laugh, and Lochlann care. There is no way she did not fear for herself as she lay with them; how could she not? She did it anyway, hoping to mend the cracks in our foundation. And maybe she had. She had certainly started to.

She had done the one thing that would set we brothers free. Not her. Never her. Under this Queen, there would never be a free Fae female. Ravena had killed Rowan anyway, freeing us if not herself. The one thing we could never do, despite our talk and desire, we could not. She had done it, and she'd had to fuck him willingly to do it.

Talk about fear. What had Ravena felt that night and every night before that in our home? The sword of Damocles hung over her every day.

That's fear.

She's the bravest person I know.

Fear is that I might never have the opportunity to make this right, for if Ari is injured, then Ravena is surely dead. She is no warrior. She is sweet, soft, kind, forgiving, just, resilient, and strong, but she is no warrior.

I kicked my horse harder. I would ride him into the ground to get to her.

We clattered through rivers, fields, and woods, never slowing. We followed the white mare on her mad dash back to her mistress. At the crossroads, our captains peeled off, continuing to follow the ghost of a horse, the rest of us thundered through the last of the roads to town.

Smoke filled the air, and the scent of the burning dead was overwhelming. Lochlann caught me, and the determination on his face mirrored mine. Finally, we slowed our horses as our reckless pace quelled by rubble and milling townsfolk. I jumped from my horse and ran to our house in the very center of town, Lochlann on my heels.

We slammed into our door only to find it barred. We pounded and kicked and demanded to be let in. I was more worried than ever. Never had we barred our doors. The biggest threat had always come from within.

Finn threw the door open, and we pushed past him, rampaging through the house despite his pleas for us to stop.

Ravena lay on her bed, pale skin marred by the swipe marks of something giant and clawed. Claw marks ran down both arms and across her torso. One claw had caught the side of her perfect face and cut down her neck. She wore no clothes but was covered across her breasts and between her legs. Her arms lay limp at her sides, and I thought her dead.

Black hair spilled around her face and fanned around her like great, black wings. She was ethereal. A sob caught in my throat, and I went to her, clutching her pale hand in mine. Her eyes popped open, then fluttered closed, and I turned to my brother with a roar, "What happened, Finn? What the fuck happened?"

"Trolls," he said and then told us the story.

I gripped her hand as he spoke. He was calm. He'd had time to process while we had not. Ravena had refused the healing potion so that others could have it. She would heal, but she would scar.

Refusing to accept that, I stormed from the house and whistled for a horse. Surprised when one came, I raced to Ari's home. She would have more; I knew it. Ravena had suffered enough. She was scarred enough from her time with us. Trolls would not add injury to her insult. I raced into the night for a potion that might not do anything but make me feel less impotent. I simply couldn't look at her as she lay there like death. I could not.

I begged, pleaded, and bargained with our Goddess to help me on my way. To let Ari's mates be home even though Finn said Ari was missing. It's not like I didn't care about that. I did. But I cared about Ravena more. She was mine. Mine. I had not even taken a chance to know her. Really know her. I would beat the doors to Ari's home down and refuse to leave until I had what I wanted. I would not be denied.

## Chapter Twenty One

## Lochlann

My breath caught in my throat as I took her in. Her skin had lost its blue undertone and matched the white of her sheets as if every drop of her precious blood had already been shed. Her chest rose and fell softly, and I could see the uneven slant to her ribs and the deep bruising along her side. They were broken.

She was broken.

A sob escaped my throat, and her eyes fluttered open again, a soft smile ghosting her lips.

"It looks worse than it is," she whispered, lacking the strength to do much else.

"She wouldn't stop. She wouldn't stop working on others until the last was dragged away," Finn said, sinking into a chair next to her bed, his head hanging low and resting on his hands. I saw the truth in the slant of his shoulders and worried even more.

"I don't understand, Finn. I don't. How could this happen? Is the Queen's intelligence that bad?" I sat on the edge of

Ravena's bed, hoping not to disturb her. Her eyes did not open again, and her chest was almost still.

"Ravena said the Trolls seemed to be targeting Ari. That once she ran, they followed. They grabbed Arlie and Teagan and escaped with them. Ari saved the others, but she is also missing." He began to cry, his shoulders shaking.

I went to him, kneeling before him, "Finn, Ravena will live, and Ari will be found. Her Huntsman is the best; he will find them all."

"I should have taken her to my shop; I wanted her there anyway. I should have insisted. Someone was watching the house after you left. I should have been more careful."

"No. No, Finn. We cannot force our will on Ravena. We can't, or we are no better than he was. It's not your fault. The blame is on whoever allowed this to happen in the first place. The blame is on the…" I stopped short of saying the Queen. I had heard the story of her arrival after the chaos, and that bell didn't ring true. In my heart, I knew this. Fear kept me from saying it.

Finn and I whispered through the night as Ravena slept. She never moved, not one muscle, and the only indication she lived was the slow rise and fall of her chest.

Rory came back later that night, his face haggard and worn. Black stubble had grown into a short beard while we had been gone, and bits of dirt and leaves clung to it. He rushed to

Ravena and placed a small green bottle to her lips, begging her to drink.

Placing his hand behind her head, he tilted it up, pouring the liquid down her throat and forcing her to swallow with his hand when she could not do it her own. He placed a second green bottle on the table beside the bed.

We watched in fascination as her color improved and the deep gashes on her arms healed, leaving only dried blood behind. The marks on her face cleared, and her eyes slowly opened. She took a deep breath for the first time, rolling over onto her side and curling in a ball, she slept. Inside, the vice that had gripped me eased.

"Saige says Laith may die; he is badly injured. Seal is hunting the lost girls. Ari went over the cliff at the crossroads," he whispered. Ravena whimpered in her sleep, and I warned Rory with my eyes. "They swear she lives, and they will find her. They swear the Queen has done this," he finished, bringing his eyes up and holding ours.

We nodded but said nothing. A heaviness settled over the room. Rory took a deep breath and went to sit next to Ravena on the bed, she curled into him with a sigh and his face shattered. Tears fell silently down his cheeks as he stared at her with a look so intense I was glad her eyes were closed, and she could not see it. Tears dripped off his chin and onto her hair. If she noticed, she pretended not to.

"What do we do?" I asked.

"We be careful. We are already interesting to the Queen. We must not be interesting," Finn said.

"Agreed." Rory wiped his eyes and moved to stand. Ravena clung to his legs, refusing to lift her head from them.

"Shhhhh, let me clean up, and I'll be back. I won't leave you. Not again." He kissed her hair and disentangled himself from her limbs.

Rory and I took turns bathing. Finn sat with Ravena as she slept, and we took a minute to let it all sink in. We had almost lost her. My hands shook as I downed a shot of Absinthe, then I downed another. I let the warmth of the drink settle into my bones.

Rory joined me at the counter and drank three shots in quick succession. His haunted eyes roamed the house, taking in the closed shutters and barred doors and windows. Finn said the house had been watched while we were gone. For our sweet and trusting brother to react this way, he must have been spooked. Very spooked.

We needed to be more careful.

"Should we see what can be done in town?" I asked. "Finn said it was mostly clear, but there may be more we can do." I watched as Rory's hand shook on the shot glass he held.

"Let it burn," he said, not looking at me. He downed the last of his Absinthe and stalked to Ravena's room.

Finn was unceremoniously shoved out the door, and it closed behind him. He chuckled as he walked to me, taking the bottle of Absinthe and tipping it up. "Well, that's a development," he said, his eyes twinkling merrily.

He reached up and ruffled the longer top of his hair, causing it to settle in a mess over his eyes. "Our Fae is stronger than we ever gave her credit for. She wouldn't stop." His merry eyes turned troubled. "She's hiding potions from us. She tucked them in the skirts of her dress. When I undressed her to tend the wounds, they were gone."

"Who cares. If she kills me, I'll have deserved it. It'll keep us on our toes," I gave him a half grin and a wink. "Adds a little excitement."

"I, myself, have had enough excitement. For a while, anyway." His smile fell, and I realized he had likely seen things he wished he hadn't. Ravena damaged was only a piece of it. Finn is no soldier. "She said she would never do that to us. Not to any of us, but the fact that the potions are missing remains."

"Eh. I'll not worry about it," I said, and I wouldn't.

"We were together that first night. We just," he paused.

"Good. That's a good thing," I interrupted in case he was feeling some sense of misplaced guilt.

"That's not what I mean, not really." The furrow of his brows deepened, and he told me about the man at the fence.

I worried. I worried that the Queen would demand we take a fourth man. I worried that there was some greater conspiracy we were missing. I worried that just when we found peace, we would lose it. I did not worry about Ravena, though, not then. She was safe with Rory; no matter what he was feeling, he would not hurt her.

## Chapter Twenty Two

### Ravena

The sound of Finn squeaking as Rory shoved him out the door woke me. I had rested enough anyway and wanted to wash the dried blood off myself. Ari's healing potion had fixed me. I appreciated Rory endlessly for going after it.

Sometimes valor has a price; I was injured more than I knew when I refused it the first time. One of those things claws had popped my lung and some of the softer organs in my belly. I would've healed, but it would have been slow going until then. Now I was fine.

Thanks to Ari. Again. Thanks to Ari for everything. She couldn't be dead. I would never accept that.

I rolled over and found Rory leaning against my door and staring at me with a burning intensity that was painful. Propping myself on my elbow, I asked, "Are you okay?"

"You're asking me if I'm okay?" he said, his eyes pinning mine.

"Yes. Are you okay, Rory?" I pushed myself to sit up, feeling the faint pull of healing muscles.

In two strides, he was on me, scooping me up and tucking me into his lap, and resting his chin on my head. "Ravena," he said, burying his nose in my hair and inhaling. "I'm fine. Of course, I am fine. How are you? I was so worried."

"Better now, thank you for getting the potion." Lifting my head, I met his eyes, placing my hand on his cheek. The soft hair from the beard he'd grown while gone tickled my palm. He leaned into me, closing his eyes.

"Ari's mate gave me these; he said you would know what to do with them." Shifting me, he pulled a thin bag from his pocket and set it on the table next to us.

"They're for…" I started.

"I don't care, Ravena. I don't. Whatever they are for doesn't matter." He slid his hands down my spine, his touch uncertain and timid.

Goosebumps dotted my skin where he touched. A thin bandeau around my breasts was all I wore, and my nipples pebbled against it, brushing his chest. "Rory," I started.

"I need to touch you. Please. I was so afraid I would never have the chance. I just. Can I touch you?" His blue eyes darkened to the color of midnight as he watched my face for an answer.

"Yes, Rory."

More gently than I could have imagined, he lay me down. He knelt over me, his legs straddling my hips. Taking the tips of his fingers, he slid them across my skin. The look of concentration on his face changed to wonder as everywhere he touched, goosebumps rose to meet him.

Keeping my eyes on his face, I watched as he explored me, never lingering long in one place. He brushed my nipples, and I closed my eyes, just for a moment. He peeled the bandeau down, exposing my breasts. Circling my nipples with his fingers, he watched as they tightened under his touch.

"Do you like that?" he asked, cocking his head.

"Yes," I said, drawing out the word in emphasis.

His hands cupped my breasts together, and his own eyes closed in response to my soft moan. He raked across them with his thumbs before trailing his hands down the curve of my waist, using his hands to circle it. He slid down, moving what little cloth shielded my sex from him. He stared at the vee between my legs, tracing the soft, black hair there with his fingers. The sensation of his light touch caused me to tighten and moisture to flow.

Inhaling my scent, he noticed the change. I lay still and let him touch what he needed to. He had never touched me before. Never. Not unless he was told to and never like this. I wasn't sure he desired women; he may not have known either until then.

His pants tented from his erection, and he brushed it with his palm, looking confused and unsure.

"I said yes, Rory. Yes, to whatever. I'm willing. Even if you aren't sure, and even if you find you must stop." I reached my hand to cup his cheek. He kissed my palm, staring at me with damaged eyes.

Taking my arm in his, he kissed down it. He kissed across my neck and up to my lips. At first, his kiss was gentle and exploring. He parted my lips and met my tongue with his. It became something more, and he devoured my mouth with his. It was frantic and wild as his hands fisted my hair, pulling me to him.

He kissed me in that sweet way you kiss for the first time, experimenting on the depth and pressure of his tongue. He bit my lower lip and my chin before returning to my mouth, kissing me until I was breathless and arching against him. He kissed down my neck again, placing his hot mouth on my nipple. He sucked it, cupping my breast. His tongue whirled the tight peak, and I moaned again.

He kissed everywhere, licked every part of me. Taking his time, he explored every inch of my body down to my toes. He took them in his mouth one at a time, not caring that I was far from clean. Not caring that there was dried blood on some of the areas he kissed. Finn had cleaned me, but I needed a bath. I was hoping once Rory was done, I would need one even more.

He was careful. Still unsure of where he was going and what he was doing. I didn't push him. I tried to keep my responses from overwhelming him. This was his choice. If he decided he wasn't that into it, he could walk away. I wouldn't let the heavy need building in my core override either of us.

When he kissed up my thighs, pushing them apart to settle between them, I changed my mind. He ran his tongue lightly over my core. Tangling my fingers in his hair, I groaned, forcing myself to hold back from riding his face like I wanted to.

Taking his fingers, he spread my lips apart and licked the thin, delicate skin around my opening. He licked everywhere, exploring me with his eyes, his lips, and his tongue. He groaned as he slipped a finger inside of me, moving it slowly in and out. Arching hard, I cried out as he covered my core with his mouth, running his tongue over it until I came against him.

Before I could finish, he moved away, pulling his shirt off and tossing his pants to the side. Between my legs, he gripped his cock, lining it up and pushing into me slowly. He watched where we were joined, his face softening. The feel of him in me for the first time drew my orgasm out, and I clenched around him. A look of surprise crossed his face before it darkened into something else.

Desire.

Desire and need rolled off of him so thick I could smell it. He lowered himself with care, taking most of his weight onto his arms, but not all. Kissing me again, he rolled his hips into me, stretching me to the limits with his girth.

My breathing came hard and fast, and after only a few thrusts, I came undone around him, crying out and gripping his back with my fingers. I came hard, feeling the clench and release of my muscles around him. With a groan, he buried his face in my neck and emptied himself deep inside me.

He shook afterward. His whole body released tension that it had long held, and I ignored the feel of his tears on my skin. We lay there, connected by arms, legs, and old, shared pain. I trailed my hands down his back, gripping the sheets to cover us.

He was asleep in no time, his fingers still tangled in my hair and his body mostly covering mine. I tried not to move; I did. Eventually, the pressure from his limbs and my bladder forced me to, despite the tightness at which he dug into my arm as I tried to rise.

"I'll be right back," I whispered in his ear before stumbling to my wardrobe for a covering.

In the washroom, I cleaned up as best I could without a bath, brushed my teeth, and returned to my room. I extinguished the torches, slipped the robe off, and eased next to Rory, hoping not to wake him. He rolled into me as I adjusted myself around him.

"I'm sorry I was so fast," he whispered in my ear.

"You were perfect," I said, pulling him to me, tucking his head under my chin so I could hold him.

"You just felt so good."

"You did too," I said, smoothing his hair and smiling into it. He smelled wonderful, like fresh dirt and dried grass. It was amazing to me, and given my magic; he smelled like home.

His lips found my nipple, taking me by surprise. My sharp intake of breath stopped him. "I'll stop. You need to rest."

"Don't. I mean. I don't want you to stop. I need to feel you too," I said as he watched my face.

He covered me again, with his body and with his kisses, for a damaged man and brawler, he moved with more care and grace than I would have dreamed. He watched my face as he drove in and out of me, his pace slow and deliberate.

I locked my legs around his back, changing the angle of his thrusts and allowing my core to rub against him. Our lips never stopped touching, not once, as we made the most gentle love I have known in my life.

He took his time. I wanted to come with him. I held off chasing my orgasm until his breaths came harder, and his thrusts faltered.

I sped my hips, writhing on him to control the contact until we broke together. His spasms drawing out my orgasm. Our deep groans mingled in the dark as we clung to one another.

This time, when we fell asleep, tangled up in limbs and sheets, we did not rise.

A sharp knock on the door roused us not long after the sun cracked the horizon. I could have slept all day. Rain had moved in, and dark clouds covered the sun's light.

Rain is rare in Talamh na Sithe. It happens just often enough to keep the crops growing, but not much more. It's like the Goddess loves the sun and only covers it when she must.

A blanket covered Rory, who still slept. I took the sheet we had kicked off during the night, wrapping it around me. Opening the door, I shut it behind me without noise so as not to wake him. When I turned, I was startled to see the Queen.

In the center of our home, she stood with her creepy goons. If I curtsied appropriately, the sheet would drop. I chose to incline my head, my eyes searching frantically for Finn and Lochlann.

They stood side by side, watchful.

"Ah, Ravena, there you are. Sorry to wake you, but I must speak to your mates, and I thought you should be here. Where is the other one? Rory, isn't it?" She didn't look sorry as she looked around the house, taking in all the changes.

She would have done a visit before my arrival to check the suitability, and the changes were many. Her goons roamed, idly opening cabinets and checking drawers, looking no doubt for poison. They had already searched the house once when Rowan died, and I'm not a stupid girl.

"He's asleep," I said.

"As he is a signatory on this contract, wake him."

Turning back to my room without a word, I closed the door behind me.

"Get dressed. The Queen is here." I shook him hard, scurrying to throw a dress over my head.

He jumped up, grabbing his pants. His face concerned but fierce. We exited the room together.

"There you are, Rory." Her eyes raked greedily down his naked chest, and my fists clenched.

Rory turned me to him, tucking me under his chin so that my back was to the Queen, and he was covered. He yawned, leaning relaxed against the wall like nothing else mattered.

From the corner of my eye, I saw her eyes narrow. "I am here to discuss the issue of adding a fourth man to your house," she said, watching our reactions closely.

Rory kissed my hair with a deep inhalation of breath to cover my gasp.

"We've been thinking about that as well, Your Highness. We've chosen one for ourselves. We were going to file a petition once the chaos had died down," Lochlann said, pushing away from the wall and walking to the couch. He patted the seat next to him, and Rory and I followed. Finn came to stand behind us, crossing his arms. "We thought we should give time for the others to heal before we asked, but since you're here."

She arched her eyebrow up, moving to sit opposite us on the chaise. Her guards moved to flank her, paying me more attention than I wanted. "Who," she asked.

"Elic. From your greenhouse," beside me, I felt Rory stiffen. Just one muscle. I doubted anyone else noticed it.

I relaxed into him. "We've become quite close now that I'm working there," I said. "Not contract breaking close, but we get on well enough. We all do. He would be a good fit and provide some much needed contrast to these dark, handsome men.

"He is not the one I would have chosen, but he is a good choice. I do want you girls to be happy so that you will produce children for me," she said, looking thoughtful. "I will consider your petition."

"And we thank you," I said before the others could pipe in and ruin it. I could feel their anger. No one wanted to produce children for the Queen; we wanted children of our own. Most of The Eight did- eventually.

I could feel rage pouring off the men and knew at that moment that they understood. Finally, they understood. They would not be angry about birth control. How could they be?

# Chapter Twenty Three

## Finn

The Queen closed the door behind her, and I slumped in my seat. We feared that she would eventually assign us another man. I never dreamed she would come the day after a Troll massacre. A day which her own daughter was still missing. She meant to keep us on edge.

I didn't care if Elic came to live with us. I just wasn't sure how Ravena would feel about having Rory's twink lover in the house. We had just found peace. She had taken Rory to her bed, and by all appearances, he was happy with the experience. He slept with her there all night. We could've settled in after that. As a family, finally. I hated to disturb our fragile peace.

But the Queen wants what she wants, and she'll get it in the end. We'll be lucky if she accepts our choice and doesn't choose for us. How can we trust her? After all, she chose Rowan.

The town was still cleaning up. We took the day off and bought lumber, stone, and finishings enough to extend our house to fit another. We would not take Ravena's room from her, and Elic, should he be accepted, would require a room of his own. We could do nothing to draw suspicion. It looked good that we are so willingly working to accommodate another.

Rory remained silent most of the day; in fact, we all did. All of us except Ravena, she chatted and smiled while we built our new addition as if it did not bother her, and maybe it didn't.

Life in Talamh na Sithe had always been this way, even though she hadn't lived long enough to see much of it. She seemed to accept it all the same. In fact, if anything, she was excited.

At times her face would drop, and I knew she worried about her sisters, but when asked, she said she wasn't afraid. They would come home. All of them. She believed it with her whole heart.

Arlie did come home. Seal and a team of huntsmen tracked her, killing the Troll and returning Arlie to her mates unharmed.

Days passed. Teagan had been tracked to the border between the Trolls and Eregion, where the Eruhini live. Origins tells us that we were once one people, the Daoine Sidhe and the Eruhini. Summer Court and Winter, but I know no one who lived in those days, and little history of the time remains.

The Queen refused to allow a strike team to rescue Teagan. Ari remained missing, and no one has seen her men since she disappeared. Rumors and speculation grow like weeds in a garden. Or rats in the streets.

We did not stay at home. We made sure we were seen around town. Happily holding hands or eating at the diner, we made our presence known. The Queen would hear nothing untoward about us. We could not afford it.

Late evening on the fifth day after the Massacre brought a knock at our door. Ravena had just placed dinner on the table, and we were desperately trying to avoid eating it. All of us jumped to answer, delaying the inevitable meal of boiled, almost jellied rabbit she was so proud of for as long as possible.

Elic stood at the door. No fanfare. No herald. Just Elic and two bags. Maybe Rory had warned him that we had petitioned for him, maybe not. He had spent these last nights with Ravena, closed in her room, not his. They stayed from dark to light. We could hear them talking long into the night. Maybe Ravena needed it; maybe Rory did. Regardless, I was grateful to them both for being there for each other.

Ravena had not seemed to suffer permanent effects from her few weeks with Rowan, but Rory had suffered horribly. We all had, but he seemed to hold onto it the longest. While my torture may have been more frequent due to my softer appearance, Rory's had cut him deeper. Maybe she could fix him. Maybe she could fix us all.

When Ravena saw Elic, her smile widened and took over her entire face. It was the most beautiful thing I had ever seen. It lit her face and made her blue eyes sparkle like precious jewels.

Wiping her hands on her apron, she went to him, throwing her arms around his neck. "Welcome, Elic, come. I will show you to your room. They have worked so hard getting it ready for you!" she said, pulling back and clapping her hands. "You boys go eat while I show Elic around, then he can eat too."

I caught his eyes and rounded mine with fear, giving desperate shakes of my head back and forth behind Ravena's back.

"Ravena, I just ate. Thank you, though. I did not want to impose as you didn't know I was coming," he said, uncertain, watching me over her head.

I sagged in relief. We would need to warn him. Ravena tries so hard, but damn if her cooking seemed to be getting worse, not better. We had taken to keeping dried meat in the woodshed and filling our bellies there after we managed to sneak our dinners out to the rats.

If Ari didn't come back, we would starve.

Ravena hooked her arm through his and guided him through the back of the house. The rest of us hurried to our plates, clicking silverware and making sounds of appreciation while we pretended to eat jellied rabbit. Then we snuck outside, scrapping our plates behind the fence. Fae rats weren't picky, but we would need to get a cat soon, or else they would multiply to a dangerous extent.

We rushed back to the table and sat, breaking up some sort of flattened bread that was missing more than one ingredient and trying to scatter it about so it would look like we had eaten it.

At some point, we would have to intervene. Rory was an excellent cook and didn't mind doing it. All of us could cook better than Ravena, but she seemed to love it.

She sang and hummed the whole time she was in the kitchen, rubbing her hands together in excitement as she went. It was sweet, really, but once she had cooked a fresh beaver before Lochlann could remove the thing's fur. She cooked it over an open flame, tail and all. I belched furry beaver for days.

Another time she boiled a large inedible fish she found at the market. This particular fish is boiled down, and the mixture used to keep Dire Wolves from eating livestock. You put it around the boundary of your field to discourage wild animals.

We'd started a small fire in the bathroom, burning the curtains to create a diversion so we could feed the fish to the rats. They hadn't touched it either, and the alley behind our house stank for days.

Something had to be done.

But tonight, we sat, spreading bread crumbs and making appreciative noises while the soft hum of Elic and Ravena talking whispered down the hall because that's what mates do. How could we hurt her like that? Someday we would figure out a way to keep her out of the kitchen. Somehow we would find another way to fill her need to take care of us, but we did what we had to so she would be happy for now.

## Chapter Twenty Four

### Ravena

I pulled Elic down the hallway, trying not to make it awkward. I was excited because I liked him. It was a little awkward because I knew he liked Rory. I also knew that Rory liked me, and I liked Rory. We all liked each other, so It would work itself out.

Elic was fast becoming one of my best friends. He fits in so well with Ari and the rest of us. We loved having a handsome man around that we could flirt with and talk to. He was fun, but more importantly, he was safe. Elic had no interest in females. None.

Finn had done Elic's room in soft greens and browns, taking a page from his love of plants for the color scheme. It was a nice room, not large, but it had a decent sized wardrobe and was close to the new washroom.

Lochlann had insisted on adding another one as five often dirty Fae sharing one was too much. Especially when I liked to linger in the bath.

He tossed his bags on the bed and looked around. "It's a nice space," he said, looking around.

"I hope you like it. I also hope that you aren't leaving behind a home you loved to come to this one," I said, sitting on the chair by his bed. Rory had made the headboard himself. It was an intricate design of carved wood and curved steel.

He leaned against it. "I lived in a small room at the Greenhouse, this is much nicer, and I won't miss it. What are the rules?" he asked, his voice an octave lower than normal and his eyes almost tired.

"There are none. Not really. You are free to be with Rory, and he is free to be with you, but he is also free to be with me. I have no hang-ups or aversions. I've learned it's better to follow the flow where life takes me. All of us want happiness.

"As long as you understand Rory may want to be with me on occasion, I will understand the same. There is no judgment here, and I am not the jealous type. We have different things to offer, you and I. We are friends, not competition," I finished, not wanting there to be any miscommunication or misunderstandings among us.

"And Rory?" he asked, his yellow eyes probing mine.

"Rory and I talked it out over the last few days. He wants you in his life. He cares for you, and he cares for me. There are no misunderstandings between us. My word to you. I know you have no desire for females, and I am fine with that. As long as we can be friends, I am happy." I smiled at him, feeling it reach my eyes and crinkle the corners.

"Okay," he said, sadness creeping across his gorgeous eyes, vanishing as quickly as it came.

"I can offer you more than friendship. I can help with the house, and I have a knack for cooking," he said, moving to unpack his bags. I rose, pulling out shirts and pants, handing them to him.

"Oh, I don't know. The brothers love my cooking; they may object to that. I've never seen Faeman eat so much. Sometimes entire pots of dinner disappear," I said, folding over another shirt. It was a delicate lilac color and the fabric finer than any I had owned. I ran my fingers over it. Business must be good at the nursery.

"You know I have no plant magic; you've seen that for yourself. My parents owned the nursery before me, and I can keep it well enough, but I have no magic for it. What I can do is cook. That is where my magic lies. Maybe you can try to teach me plant magic, and I can teach you cooking magic. It will make your amazing meals even better," he said, giving me a smile that did not quite reach his eyes.

"Deal," I said, leaving him to finish settling in alone. He might need time to adjust to his new space.

In the kitchen, Lochlann, Rory, and Finn were clearing the table and washing dishes. Crumbs littered the floor, and empty plates were stacked by the sink.

"How did it go?" Rory asked, turning to face me. His eyes clouded with worry.

"Just fine, Rory, stop worrying." I went to him, standing on my tiptoes to kiss his cheek. Surprising me, he gripped my waist tightly and kissed my lips, dipping his tongue to mine.

He had never touched me in front of his brothers. We had spent the last few days sequestered in my room, making love and talking for hours. He had been unsure about his sexual feelings toward women until we slept together and after he felt he had some catching up to do. I laughed about it, knowing the others would understand.

Rory loved Elic and had for years. He was worried that Elic would not understand and that I would be jealous. I assured him that I would be fine and Elic would adjust. Rory and I had a lifetime to find love together or not. His gigantic size and calloused hands belied the fact that he is a gentle and generous lover. I wanted things to grow between us naturally and hoped they would, for that reason, and many others.

I watched as he walked away toward Elic's room. Smiling, I turned to Lochlann and Finn. "Let's walk to the diner and have dessert," I said, reaching for their hands.

"Excellent idea," Lochlann said, tripping over his feet in his rush to get to an apple pie. As good as my cooking is, I am no baker. In Ari's absence, Miri, the old Fae from the diner, had begun making pies and cakes. They were not as good as Ari's, but they would do until she got back.

They walked so quickly I stumbled to keep up. If I had known how badly they missed Ari's cakes and cookies, I would have tried to bake some for them, but in my heart, I knew that she was coming home. By the time I got my baking up to par, she would be back, and it would be a moot point.

They barged in the diner, grabbing menus for themselves. My dinner had been interrupted by Elic's arrival, and I was starved. The brothers had it all cleaned away when I was finished talking to him, and I had missed it.

"Miri, I'll have the seared duck with a slice of apple pie," I said when she came to take our order. I was happy to see that she was completely healed from her run-in with the Trolls.

"Make that two of those," Finn said, putting his menu down and smiling at me. "Rabbit just doesn't sit long; I could use another plate before I have to deal with you tonight." He gave me a rakish wink and cocked a smile at Miri.

"Make that three plates and three pies," I could use a little extra energy too." Lochlann smiled, and I laughed at them. They loved coming in here and stirring up speculation about our match.

It was adorable.

"Ravena," Miri turned back to me after starting to walk away. "You should come and work part-time for me. I could use extra help in the kitchen." She gave me a kind smile.

Lochlann choked on his water, his eyes watering.

"Don't gulp, Lochlann," she said, narrowing her eyes at them both.

Finn's face had paled, and I wondered why.

"I already have a job two days a week at the nursery. My magic has an affinity for plants, so that's a good fit for me," I answered, not wanting to say no to her.

"That's even better; I grow most of the vegetables and herbs I use here. It would be an asset to have them tended by you. How about helping cook for the lunch crowd two days a week. I could really use it." She placed her hands on her back, stretching it out. This place probably was a lot of work for her. It was always packed.

From the corner of my eye, I saw Finn shaking his head, swatting at something frantically. "Are you okay, Finn?" I asked.

"Fine, yes, fine. There was a…fly. A very large and bitey fly. I was trying to shoo it."

Rolling my eyes, I turned away from him. "I think I would enjoy that, Miri. I'm a good cook. I could help you. The brothers can't get enough of it."

Finn inhaled the fly, his eyes turning red. Poor man. He drank his water to the bottom, waiting patiently as Miri refilled it. "Perfect," she said. "Could you be a dear and go around back and see if you can perk up my plants, they are quite wilted."

"I would love to." I walked around the back to do just that.

## Chapter Twenty Five

### Rory

I heard the front door shut and knew the others had left, giving Elic and me some time alone. Well, and to go eat. Goddess, I hope my brothers threw away every scrap of that congealed looking rabbit.

I changed into pajamas then went to find Elic. He was sitting in his room, staring at the wall.

"Hey," I said from his doorway.

"Hey," he answered.

"Rule number one. Don't eat anything Ravena cooks if you can help it. Follow our lead; we'll show you how to avoid it without hurting her feelings. She seems to love to cook, but she is quite terrible at it." I felt like that needed saying first and foremost.

"It can't be that bad," he said, grinning up at me.

"Oh, it can. It most certainly can. There is dried and salted meat hidden in the woodshed. There's enough there to keep us from starving until we figure out how to nicely tell her to find a new hobby. May I?" I asked, nodding to his bed.

"Sure." He tilted his head to indicate I should come in, drawing his legs up to his chest and hugging them. "This is weird," he finished, looking around the room.

"The room is weird?" I asked, knowing what he meant.

"No. Not the room. The room is nice." He tucked his legs under himself. He was restless and seemed uncomfortable. "This is weird." He waved his hand to the space between us.

"It won't be. Not for long," I said, patting the space beside me on the bed. "Ravena's capacity to care is deep, and to understand is endless. We think it is part of her magic that she may not be aware of. She's incredibly kind and generous, despite her beginnings here."

I watched Elic's silver hair catch the light from the torches as he slid from the chair to the spot next to me. "She said she doesn't care. Not about us. Not about any of it," he said, laying his head on my shoulder. "I've missed you."

"I've missed you too," I said, resting my hand in his hair. "And she means it. She doesn't care. Not even a tiny bit. She just wants all of us to be safe and find peace, and she knows I care for you. She is more than happy to share if you are." I let my hand tangle in his hair.

"For the first time, Rory, we have an opportunity to be together without Rowan beating us down. I can live with that. I can live with whatever it takes for you and me to be safe." He angled from me, catching me with his odd, yellow eyes. "What happened, Rory? What happened to him?"

"The examiner said he must have had a heart defect that no one knew about. His heart just stopped," I said, meeting his eyes with my own.

What I said was the truth. His heart had stopped. I might love Elic, but the secret of that night would die with the four who knew it. It wasn't a trust issue so much as a binding promise made. We brothers had sworn to tell no one, even after our suspicions were confirmed. The Goddess had accepted our promise. I couldn't speak of it if I wanted to.

"No poison?" he asked, canting his eyes at me.

"Ravena's cooking is awful, but no one has died from eating it. I swear." I chuckled, changing the subject.

He sank to his knees on the floor in front of me, undoing the string on my pajamas. I watched as he took me into his mouth. It was sudden, and my cock lay limp on his tongue. He bobbed his head along my shaft, and it grew harder. Tangling my hands in his hair, I let out a low groan.

His expert tongue caressed me, his fingers finding every spot he knew I loved. One slipped into me, and I bit back a cry, pulling him to me. I had enjoyed every moment with Ravena. Every single one, but I enjoyed this too. Elic had held my heart for a long time; being with him was familiar and comforting.

I took his clothes, tossing them to the side as I wrenched my pajamas off. He reached into the drawer beside his bed, pulling out oil and rubbing it on my cock. His fingers squeezed at the perfect pressure, and my eyes closed, but I didn't want to be nice. I didn't want to be gentle.

Not tonight.

"Get on your knees, Elic," I ordered. His eyes darkened, and he did as I said.

Behind him, I angled my oiled cock and pushed hard and fast into him, causing him to cry out. I didn't want to be careful, so I took him in a way I could never take Ravena. At least not yet.

Gripping his hips, I pumped into him at a punishing pace. His head fell onto his chest, and his cries echoed my own. Taking his hair, I forced his head back, arching his neck, and gave what I needed to give, knowing he would love it. Elic didn't like gentle. Not often.

When I knew I couldn't hold back anymore, I let his neck go, grabbed his cock, and fisted it hard until he shuddered under me, emptying on the bed below him. I followed, filling him as I moaned. We collapsed, breathing hard.

I hadn't kissed him in ages, so I kissed him now. He tasted like fennel, smelled like it too. His tongue danced with mine. He hadn't forgotten, and neither had I. Our rhythm was practiced and perfect. I smiled into his mouth, and he smiled back. I rose, grabbing a towel, and cleaned myself off. I threw it to him, blew out the torches, and curled with him on his bed.

"You'll stay?" he said, the sound of surprise clear in his voice.

"Do you not want me to stay?" I asked.

"No, I do," he answered. Adjusting himself around me.

"Then I'll stay." Despite the early hour, I was asleep in no time.

# Chapter Twenty-Six

## Lochlann

"You can't mean to let her cook in your diner, Miri. You have no idea what you're getting into," I said, clutching the small woman's apron in a panicked plea.

"It can't be that bad, Lochlann," she said, putting both hands on her hips and glaring at me.

"It can, it really can," I said, the last words coming out in a whimper.

"Oh, I've seen you feed the alley rats often enough. Maybe the poor girl will learn to be better at it. Maybe this job is what she needs.

"She'll chase away all your patrons," Finn said in no uncertain terms.

"You boys quit exaggerating," she said, stomping away to make our supper.

"Miri will learn in due time, or maybe Ravena can learn." my eyes popped to Ravena as she came to a stop behind him.

"Learn what?" she said, her eyes narrowing on me.

"Learn to take us both tonight," he whispered in her ear, causing her cheeks to redden prettily. "We've felt left out these last few nights."

"Have you now?" she said, her voice light and breathy.

"We have." Finn winked at me, and I thought what an ass he was, but, Goddess, he was also brilliant. And not lying. Not at all. We had felt a little left out while she and Rory fucked liked rabbits these last few days.

Ravena sat at the head of the table, with me on her left and Finn on her right. We ate, taking our time. There was no rush. Rory and Elic needed a few minutes alone to talk through this most recent development in our lives. We ate pie and drank a few cups of ale. The pie was good and the ale better.

Ravena laughed at everything we said, her eyes sparkling in the light of the torches. She held our hands and seemed the happiest I had ever seen her.

Only when we left and passed Ari's bakery did she grow quiet. "She's coming home. I know it," she said, pressing her face against Ari's repaired bakery window. "I would feel it if she were gone. Wouldn't I?" She turned to me with tears in her eyes.

"Seal will find her. He will. There is none better." I took her in my arms, wrapping her up.

We walked the last few feet back to the house in silence, Finn on one side and me on the other. The house was dark when we entered. Finn barred the door behind us, and Ravena glanced at Elic's closed door with a soft smile.

Well, who's room will it be then?" she asked, giving a naughty little wink of her blue eye.

"Ravena, we didn't mean what we said at the diner," Finn said, brushing a kiss into her hair.

"You didn't?" she asked, arching an eyebrow.

"I mean. No? Uh, yes?" He gave her a guilty grin, ducking his head.

He had missed her, and he did mean it, but we didn't want to push.

"I told Elic that there were no rules," she said, unwrapping the light cloak she had around her shoulders. "I've been thinking about it, and I mean it. I don't want any of us to have rules." She finished with her cloak and started on the ties of her dress. "I want you to stop being afraid of me. I am not fragile, I'm not, and I'm not broken. We've all healed well enough, and time will take care of the rest," she said, dropping the dress to her ankles as my eyebrows hit my hairline. "If you want something, stop being afraid of it," she finished, walking to Finn in nothing but a pretty hair ribbon.

"Ravena," Finn started.

"Ravena, what?" she asked, bringing her lips to his.

"Ravena, nothing." He scooped her up, and she giggled, kicking her little feet and holding her hand to me.

He took her to her room and dumped her on the bed. She giggled again, scooting back until she hit her headboard. We would need to buy her a bigger bed.

Somehow, someway, the room that was meant to be her sanctuary from us had become our sanctuary with her. After staying away from it for so long, we all gravitated to it now, wanting her there more than anywhere else. She didn't seem to mind.

I had my clothes off before Finn and pounced on her like a cat, flattening her beneath me as she squealed. "You'll wake Rory and Elic," she whisper yelled.

"I doubt we will wake them. Either they sleep sated, or they are awake like we are," I said, smiling into her face and feeling the stirrings of…something, I couldn't be sure what.

"No rules?" Finn asked, tossing the last of his clothes aside. "Are you sure?"

"I am." Her smile was so big that I believed her. At that moment, she felt safe, but what about the next?

"If you become afraid, just say the word, and we will stop. If you have any fear or flashbacks, say stop, and we will." I said, holding her with my body and with my eyes.

"I will, I swear." She arched her hips into me, and I wondered at how well the naughty little minx had adjusted to everything.

"In that case, move over Lochlann; I want some too. I have been *so* lonely and felt *so* left out these last few days," he said, trying to play the guilt card.

Ravena pushed at me and rolled her eyes, not buying it but giving into me anyway. I dragged her up to her knees and positioned myself behind her while Finn pulled the hair from her face and guided her mouth to his cock. She took it eagerly, and I wondered if given a chance whether she might like it. She groaned around his length, and I knelt behind her, frozen at the sight. I had never seen anything more beautiful, and she seemed to like his cock in her mouth just fine.

She watched as Finn's eyes closed and smiled when his head dropped back. Moved by the sight, I slipped a finger inside her. She was soaked, and I knew. I knew she did like this and was not afraid. I eased another finger in, pulling the wetness with me as I drew out, circling them around her swollen nub.

She groaned around Finn, causing him to moan harder. His eyes opened, and he met mine. The look on his face was soft and enraptured. He closed his eyes slowly, his fingers resting in her hair. Unable to wait, I pushed into her, watching her sides expand with a deep breath.

I held her there for a minute as I strummed the core of her. Wetness seeped out, soaking my balls and making them tighten. I wouldn't last. No way. Not like this. I hit her cervix hard, flicking my fingers across her until she lost pace on Finn's cock and came undone. He took over, pumping into her mouth as he came, filling it, and I watched her throat as she swallowed him down. I stroked into her twice more and finished, clutching her hips and pushing into her as far as possible.

Finn pulled her off of me and settled her into his lap, her legs wrapped around him. Burying his face in her neck, he rocked her side to side. No one said anything. Not a word. I got up, blew out her torches, and tucked us all in. We placed her in the middle and boxed her in with our bodies.

She sighed with contentment, nuzzling into my chest and placing her rear in his groin. Both our arms wrapped around her, and we slept until Finn impaled her during the night, mumbling excuses about the dangers of waking someone while sleep fucking. She laughed and sank into him.

I held her as they moved on their sides, his pace slow and steady. Kissing her, I swept my hand between her legs and drew lazy circles on her core unit I brought her. She gripped me in her hand, pulling my cock base to tip, and we all came together, my seed covering her stomach, my lips and tongue on hers, with Finn's hands on her waist, his face buried in her neck.

We slept in. We pulled ourselves from my bed, bathing off the night, before going to drink the tea and eat the eggs Elic and Rory had left behind.

They were gone by the time we forced ourselves to leave the confines of the house. We held hands, with Ravena in the middle, as we walked through the town, taking our time and enjoying the warm spring morning. I kissed her goodbye at the armory while Finn continued on with her to the nursery. I stood and watched them go.

Rory and Elic walked side by side across the field far ahead of me. They did not touch and did not appear to be in deep conversation, but they did appear fluid and relaxed together. They waved goodbye as they parted, Rory heading inside for his assignment and Elic heading towards the nursery. At the last minute, he changed his mind and headed back into town at a brisk pace. He had probably forgotten something at the house. No doubt, he wasn't sure which way was up at this point.

I hoped he settled and was happy with us. It had to be an adjustment for him and might take some time, but it was a good thing in the end if it protected us all.

## Chapter Twenty Seven

### Ravena

I hugged Finn goodbye and sighed as he walked away, tossing his shaggy bangs back and grinning at me as he left. Something had changed for all of us, and I took it as a good sign coinciding with Elic's arrival. We had done the right thing, and now we could settle in and find our little slice of happiness and peace.

I feel like my plan had worked, but maybe it was simply timing that had caused life and the brothers to settle. The sword that hung over our necks no longer seemed ever-present. I had hidden the black bottle I found in Ari's bakery well, and there was no chance of anyone finding it. I assumed her mates had done the same.

Wherever Ari was, she was safe, and I wasn't going to fear for her. I knew of her plans to become Queen, and maybe she ran until she could make that happen. She lived, and I knew it. We were just that close. I hummed as I walked, feeling happiness settle deep into my core.

Elic was not inside when I slid the large doors open. It looked as if he had not been there this morning, even though he left long before we did. I opened window curtains, watered, and touched all the plants in preparation to open for business.

He ran through the door just as the first customers arrived. "Ravena, I didn't think you would be coming in today," he said, stopping short when he saw me.

"I'm glad I did, or you wouldn't be ready to open," I said, laughing at him and waggling my eyebrows. "You two must have made a pit stop along the way. Do tell." I sat down my watering can and planted my chin on my hands in anticipation.

"Oh. Yes," Elic laughed, flipping his hair back. "I couldn't help myself, but I'm not saying anything else. Actually, I forgot something and had to run, literally, back to get it. This move was so sudden, and I have no idea where anything is anymore," he laughed, ducking behind a door at the far end of a row of plants. I had never really paid attention to it before; it must have led to his old rooms.

When he came out, he had cleaned up and changed clothes. The day was busy, and he sold so many plants I had to see to the sprouts at the back of the greenhouse so that he would have plenty of plants for the following days

I suspected the townsfolk were coming in to catch a glimpse of the two of us. We made a show of bending our heads together and whispering to fan the flames of gossip but did not go so far as to kiss or touch.

Anyone watching would see that we got along well, and the joy we found in being together wasn't faked. We hoped word would get back to the Queen that all was well and that the matching had at last settled in the way she hoped.

I left when the sun was high in the sky, heading to the diner to see if Miri needed help before I went home. Despite my protests, she gave me food for the evening meal and asked me to come in for the lunch crowd the next day.

At home, I washed clothes and changed sheets, opening the windows to the warm spring day. The need for nightly fires would soon pass, and we would swelter in the heat of the place, so for now, I would enjoy the cool breeze lifting the curtains.

I lit candles, freshened flower arrangements, and swept the floors until they gleamed. Then I slipped into my bedroom and refreshed my lip stain and eye kohl. The brothers had said nothing about my makeup, and so I snuck a little more each day. Today I dusted my face with white powder to try and reduce the blue cast. It seemed to be growing a little darker lately, probably from being out in the sun.

Finally, I changed clothes and sat in the garden with a good book, waiting for my mates to come home as anticipation coursed through me. I felt so light and free inside that it was hard to sit still and be patient, but I managed. Just barely.

## Chapter Twenty Eight

### Finn

Something wasn't right. I watched as Rory meandered through the market on his way home. Initially intent on catching up to him, I had hung back when I noticed he was being tailed by the Queen's notorious guards.

They were good. I wouldn't have noticed they were following him if Rory hadn't stopped abruptly to pick up some trinket, causing them to fall back. It was evident after that. While he shopped, picking up more things Ravena didn't need, they sat on a bench by the fountain in the middle of the square looking out of place. As he went, they ghosted behind him and me behind them.

Ravena was outside caring for her landscaping when Rory strolled up behind her, plucked her off her feet, and carried her over his shoulder like a neanderthal. She squealed, smacking at his backside as she swayed behind him, her long, black hair dragging the ground.

The guards ducked down the alley, and I hurried to cut them off, wondering if they were the ones watching the night Ravena and I were in the garden. I wondered what they were after.

As they came behind the back of the bakery, I cut them off. "Did you see the size of that rat?" I asked, waving a stick about like a wild man. "It was huge! I mean gigantic! What in the name of all that's Fae are they feeding those things?" I waved the stick at the rat I never saw. Not this time, anyway.

"We saw no rats," the light-haired one said, turning on his heel to go. The dark one followed, and they left with curious glances backward. Whether they knew they'd been caught or not, I can't say. I needed to talk to my brothers.

Rory was home early, and from the sounds of the squeals coming from Ravena's room, he was in a good mood. So was she. Her bed groaned from the force of whatever they were doing, and their moans could be heard from the front door. Closing it behind me, I walked down the hall and leaned against her door frame, watching as he drove between her legs. He took her mouth with his, covering her cries. It was a beautiful thing, seeing them together and our family whole again.

I watched for a minute, thinking how lucky we were, how lucky we all were, to have each other. I left them with a smile and went to the kitchen, intent on saving us from her cooking tonight. Only dinner was already on the counter, stacked neatly in a large box.

I took the bowls and bags Miri must have sent and separated them out, pulling plates and glasses from the shelves to have ready. I uncorked a bottle of absinthe and took a shot, leaving the bottle out so the others could join in.

Lochlann came in not long after me, took in the happy sounds coming from down the hall, and grinned.

"Spar with me?" he asked, a glint in his eye.

"Me? I'm a lover, not a fighter. Your sparring partner is otherwise occupied," I said, my lips curving up into a smile.

"Oh, come on. It will be fun," he said, cracking his knuckles. His grin growing larger.

"Fine. Don't mess up my face; it's my best feature." I stripped my shirt off and tossed it on the couch before heading out to the garden.

I watched as Lochlann tossed his shirt next to mine and joined me. His muscled chest twitched and moved in ways mine never would, making me feel puny. His biceps were like small mountains and hard as stone. He's a big son of a bitch. What was I thinking? We aren't little boys anymore. "Rory was followed on the way home today," I said, putting my fists up in front of my face. It really is my best feature. I'd hate to mess it up.

"What?" he said, dropping his guard and his fists. I clocked him with a right hook, earning a feral grin and a narrowing of his eyes.

"The Queen's guards followed him; I trailed behind and intercepted them in the alley. I chased them away under the guise of looking for rats. There are consistently rats in that alley, only now they seem to be of the Faeman variety." I ducked left and then right under Lochlann's next two jabs.

"Why would they be following any of us? It doesn't make sense," he said, catching me on the chin lightly before I could duck away.

"I don't know. Someone was watching the house while you were away. Maybe they are still curious about Rowan?" I asked, landing another jab to his cheek with my left hook. It was unlike me to land a single blow on Lochlann; his head wasn't in it.

"There's nothing to find. It was a horrible circumstance. Father had a weak heart too; maybe he inherited it," he said, his eyebrows dropping so low as to almost obscure his eyes.

We never speak the truth about Rowan's death. We know. We whispered about it behind closed doors in the dark of night but never, ever spoke about it during the light of day.

"Of course, I'm often afraid the same end will befall those of us that remain. The body on our little minx could stop the heart of an Ogre," he added, dodging my clumsy uppercut and landing one of his own. I tasted blood on my lip.

"That's true enough. She's been rather wild lately; if it were going to happen, it would have," I said, licking my lip with my tongue. The sharp smell of copper scented the air around us.

When we were little, we loved rolling around and fist fighting. We never meant it, at least not Lochlann, Rory, or I. Leaning back to avoid his right jab, I drove my shoulder into his torso, taking his breath and riding him to the ground. I hopped up and resumed my fighting stance, my fists guarding my face. "Any word on Ari?" I asked, watching him pop back to his feet.

"No. Nothing. Her mates are still sequestered. Lann threatened to take the Queen's head, and the others have kept him away from town. None of them have reported for duty since she was taken," he answered, his eyes growing dark with worry.

What would we do without our beautiful Fae? A shiver ran through me. "They'll find her. Ravena believes that." I landed another punch, jerking Lochlann's head back. He followed with a one-two punch to my gut, bending me over. "Mercy," I said, clutching my waist and trying to catch my breath.

"You're hopeless." He ruffled my hair and laughed as he stood, watching me struggle to breathe.

"I told you I'm a lover, not a fighter." My eyes watered, and my breath caught in my throat.

"So you did." He moved to sit on a stone bench by our fence. "There are whispers about where she could have gone. If she were dead, the Huntsman would have found her body. We just need to keep our heads below the Queen's eye level, and all will be well. Wherever Ari is, she is safe. Her mates will take care of her."

"And Ravena? She loves her as family." I sat next to him, our shoulders touching.

"And we take care of Ravena. She will be okay; we will make sure of it." Pushing up, he walked inside, looking over his shoulder to wait on me. I followed, not liking what he said but understanding why he said it.

We couldn't afford to be interesting. Not even a little bit.

The sun was setting, and soft yellow light filtered through the kitchen glass. Rory stumbled into the hallway with a pained groan and shut the door to the washroom to clean up. Ravena must have been in the other one as the sound of twin baths being drawn echoed through the quiet of the kitchen.

I plated food for our evening meal, marveling at the fact that it was all still warm. I wonder if that was Miri's magic. Magic is an unusual thing. Ours is weak but useful in little ways like this. Gone are the days when Fae were strong and magic stronger. We're just barely hanging on. Growing plants, shooting straight, and keeping food warm was about all we had. Maybe it's a good thing. Too much power creates difficulties none of us need.

Only I hated the thought of losing our magic entirely, and that may be the case if things were allowed to deteriorate further. What if the magic leaving the land meant we also lost our near immortality? I wondered what that would mean as I listened to bath waters run.

Rory came out first, water dripping down his shirtless chest and a sly grin on his face. "Have you seen Elic?" he asked.

"Not since this morning," I said through a mouthful of chicken and buttery mashed potatoes.

"It's just now dark," Ravena said, popping up behind him and kissing his cheek. "He'll be along soon, worry wort." She grabbed her plate and began devouring it with post-sex gusto. I loved seeing her this way.

Her wet, black hair lay straight at her hips. She never cut it, not that I could see, but she kept her bangs so that they just dusted her brows, making her blue eyes pop. She had put on lip stain again; she always does. She thinks she is sneaking it in, but none of us care, not like Rowan did. She could paint her beautiful face any way she liked, and we wouldn't blink. We're just happy she's happy.

The white of her shift brought out the blue tint on her shapely, muscular legs, and I hurried through my dinner. I was going to ruin her bath in spectacular fashion. She caught my heated glance and winked at me. Goddess, how things had changed.

## Chapter Twenty Nine

## Lochlann

Elic came through the door, parcels in hand, kicking it closed behind him. "I got you all a few things to show my appreciation for accepting me into your house so completely." Elic dropped his bags on the couch and went to kiss Ravena and then Rory on the cheek.

I didn't trust him.

I didn't trust any of this.

Nothing good is ever easy, and this was too easy.

I said nothing. The others seemed so happy and at ease that I didn't want to ripple their calm. Mistrust is like a rock on the surface of a pond, the waves of it continue and have no end, so I kept my thoughts to myself.

Rory seemed to have forgotten just how complicated his relationship with Elic was. Elic was high maintenance and demanding. It was his constant need to be acknowledged by Rory that got Rory raped and beaten within an inch of his life by Rowan, who did not tolerate anyone else in our lives but himself. He barely tolerated us touching Ravena and Ravena touching us and only did so because she was a new toy to him.

He would have broken her eventually for it.

I'm grateful every day that she killed him.

But Rory has forgotten his past with Elic. It's like he doesn't remember how hard Elic pushed. It was almost like he enjoyed drawing Rowan's ire. He's a little shit-stirrer that one. Their relationship had needed to remain a secret, and Elic did a good job of not allowing that to happen.

We had all had relationships that Rowan didn't know about. At least, I think we did. We kept them quiet, so it's hard to say, but with Rory and Elic, the secret was poorly kept. And not because of Rory. Rory almost paid the ultimate price for Elic's vanity.

Something did change after the last beating, the one that almost took Rory from us forever. Maybe Elic learned and truly is happy about being here. Maybe he was fine sharing Rory with Ravena. Maybe. Time would tell, but I would watch to be sure he could be trusted. He was never happy sharing before, and something told me he wouldn't be now. We had already suffered enough.

Ravena took her gift, holding it up for us to see. It was a bracelet with a center stone so deep a blue as to be almost purple. I had never seen anything like it before. She squealed as he put it on her wrist, hugging him to her. "I'll never take it off!" she said.

I stood back, watching as parcels were opened and smiles and laughter exchanged. Beware of men bringing gifts, I thought as he handed me my own parcel. Giving him a smile that assuredly did not reach my eyes, I opened it.

On a nest of thin paper lay an original copy of *Illuminations of the Fae Mind*. This book, alone, would have cost a fortune, more than what the keeper of a modest greenhouse should be able to afford. Add in the other gifts, and the sum was staggering. The book was bound in the softened green skin of some lesser Fae creature and leafed in gold. I was afraid to touch it.

"I traded the book dealer a year's worth of plants for it. With Ravena around, it cost me nothing. I know you like to wrap your mind around philosophic and esoteric things," he said, clapping me on the back and going back to sit with Ravena on the couch.

We sat in the living room and talked about everything and nothing. When the food was gone and the lamps burned low, I rose, stretching to go to my room. I had intended to ask Ravena to stay with me there, but Elic was braiding her hair so intently, and she looked so relaxed that I let it go.

She said they were friends and that she liked him, that he fits in so well with the girls, and she hoped their friendship would grow. I had tried to caution her about him, but she wouldn't hear of it.

Maybe I was wrong. Maybe he just wanted friendship and others to share his life with. I hoped that was it. I really did. I kissed her cheek and ran my fingers down her face before heading to the bath and my bed.

Their voices trickled in through the night, their laughter deep and muffled. It lulled me to sleep in a way nothing else could. Our house had never known so much laughter, not in the long time that this family had inhabited it.

Drifting in and out of sleep, I listened as their voices rose and fell until they wound down to quiet whispers. When the hour was late, I heard them separate and head to bed. Someone ducked into the bath, likely Finn, since he was the only one yet to bathe, and he would need to get the blood from our sparring off before going to sleep.

Rory's torches lit, and his bed creaked. I listened as Elic whispered to Ravena outside my door, bringing me to an alert state.

"You can hang out in my room tonight if you want," Elic said to her. "Might be nice to give your vagina a break."

"Would my vagina be getting a break?" she chuckled at him.

"Gods yes, no offense. Your vagina is perfectly safe with me. Your hair, however, is not. I've got an idea for another braid I'd like to try. Let's have a sleepover," he said, his voice rising a notch.

"A sleepover?" she asked.

"Yes. Stay in my room. We'll talk all night and confuse everyone in the morning when they wake up and find us together," he said with a hint of something in his voice.

"I don't want to upset them," she said.

"Oh, come on. You'll not upset them. They'll be glad we are getting on so well. It makes us all safer," he finished.

"I suppose it does. I'll get my pillow." I heard her footsteps as she walked away.

Sliding from my bed, I went into the hallway. Ravena had left her door open, and her bed was indeed empty. We rarely closed our doors since there was no point in it. Finn was heading from the bathroom, and I put my finger over my lips to shush him before easing down the hall to listen outside Elic's door.

Laughter and whispers slid like smoke through the air. He asked her simple things. Girl talk things like which one of us she prefers and who has the bigger cock. Ravena just laughed, never giving him a straight answer. She said she had no favorites. My shoulders eased at the line of their conversation, and I had considered leaving when a stray phrase caught my ears.

Poison.

He asked her about Ari making poison. Ravena laughed it off, but as the conversation tended toward things we should never speak of, I knocked on the door.

"Ravena, I hate to pull you away, but Finn is having a nightmare, and I can't wake him." I waved my hands at Finn, and he tiptoed at a run to his room to fake a nightmare.

Funny that he had no idea what was going on but went with it anyway. "You have the magic to break these things. Will you come?" I finished.

"Finn? Having a nightmare?" she asked, rising quickly. It was usually Rory that had them the worst, but we all got them from time to time.

She was up and out of Elic's room without pause; I followed with a quick shrug of my shoulders as an apology to him. I shut his door as I went, discouraging him from following.

In Finn's room, she plastered herself to his back, rocking him without a word. He was still damp from his bath, and she either did not notice or did not care. He caught my eye and glared at me. Trying to convey with a look that I would explain later, I blew his torches out and slid into bed behind her so that we sandwiched her in.

She said she was giving her vagina a rest, so I snuggled in, trying to fall immediately to sleep and failing. When their breathing slowed, and soft snores sounded, I rolled over. Laying awake the rest of the night with nothing to do but think.

## Chapter Thirty

### Rory

What the Fuck. When I went to sleep, Ravena and Elic were snuggled in his room, braiding each other's hair or some shit, and I was in my bed alone. Funny turn of events, that. I smiled as I drifted off. Ravena had drained me anyway, or had I done that to myself? With her, I can't be sure.

When I woke up, Elic was snuggled against me, and Ravena was nowhere to be found. I'd like to have them both in bed, but I'm not sure any of us are there yet. I'd have to figure out how to work that since that would mean Elic would have to top me, something we didn't normally do. I might be able to be talked into it. He probably could be too.

I rose, peeling myself away so as not to wake him. I walked past Finn's open door heading to the kitchen only to stop and back up. Finn, Ravena, and Lochlann lay piled up in Finn's bed in a tangle of arms and legs. Her blue skin stood out against their smooth white even as their black hair twined as one solid, lovely mass on his soft cream sheets.

Scratching my head and trying to figure out exactly what happened last night, I went to the kitchen to put on a pot of water for tea. I even made breakfast so that none of us had to eat Ravena's cooking.

After breakfast was finished, I went back down the hall to dress. Ravena didn't have to work today, that I knew, but Elic did. I was headed to wake him when I walked down the hall and found him in Ravena's room instead of his own, looking through one of her drawers.

"Here it is!" he said when he saw me.

"Here what is?" I asked, moving to sit on her empty bed.

"This is the loveliest hairpin I have ever seen; last night she said I could use it and told me it was in her drawer," he said, moving to sit by me.

He opened his fingers, and on his palm, there was indeed a beautiful metal and glass hairpin in the shape of a hummingbird, its yellow and green wings accented with shimmering glass. Finn's work, to be sure.

"It is lovely," I said, leaning in to kiss him. "Just like you," I said, watching his cheeks blush prettily.

"I want to braid this into her hair today; it will be stunning," he said against my lips, winking at me as he popped up and walked down the hall, leaving me sitting on Ravena's bed wondering what in the world was actually happening.

I could hear my brothers in the kitchen, and I followed the sound of their hushed conversation. It stopped when I came around the corner.

"Good morning, brother. How did you sleep?" Finn asked, his bright blue eyes shining.

"I don't exactly know," I said, taking a plate and piling it high with toasted bread and scrambled eggs. Someone had mixed cheese into them, and I groaned when they hit my tongue. Definitely an improvement over my plain eggs. "Where's Ravena?"

"She's still asleep," Lochlann laughed, watching my eyes close in pleasure at my first bite. He must have added the cheese.

"Plans for the day?" I asked.

"I'm finishing the window I made for the house then taking a few days off. The shop has been doing well, but I need a break from all the catching up I've had to do," Finn said, piling more cheesy eggs onto his plate.

"The Queen will have us doing something dumb somewhere. Yesterday it was cleaning out an invasion of fanged butterflies from her gardens at the palace. Today? Who knows," Lochlann said between bites. "You?" he asked.

"There's a blessing of unicorns a few towns over that need to be chased off," I said with a shudder. Why a group of those mean things is called a blessing, I will never know.

"I do not envy you that," Finn said, sipping his tea and rubbing his full belly.

We talked as we ate and then cleaned up our plates. It was almost time to leave when Ravena and Elic came down the hall, whispering and laughing together in the way of friends.

Her hair was braided and piled on the top of her head most magnificently. I had never seen anything like it, and when she turned her head, I could see the hummingbird pin nesting in the back of the design. It was beautiful.

Her face was painted in an extraordinary way. Her lips were stained a soft red this morning, and her lashes covered heavily in some kind of paint that made them look longer and darker, and her cheeks were painted a deeper blue as opposed to pink. It was stunning. She looked like a goddess in a long gauzy dress, the color of mist.

"What are your plans today?" I asked, my voice breaking.

She smiled at me, noting my reaction to her. "I'm going to Miri's for the lunch crowd, but beyond that, I have no plans."

"Miri's? For lunch?" Finn gulped, and I knew we would all be having lunch at Miri's. A very long lunch that would likely last the entirety of Ravena's workday that I didn't know she had in the first place.

"Yes, dears," she laughed, tilting her head back to bare her slender neck. I planned on kicking some unicorn ass quickly. I wouldn't say a word, but it wasn't safe to leave Ravena looking like a goddess and without at least one of her mates to watch for danger.

Females are so rare it wouldn't take much for this one to get taken from us. The Troll incident proved that, and I did not want to leave Ravena alone at the diner without even Elic to watch her back. It was a real eye-opener. He watched us watch her, and a smile curved on his lips. He had settled in so perfectly, and it made me happy.

"What are you doing until lunch?" Finn asked, slanting his eyes in her direction.

"I thought I would walk through town and see if anyone has any news on Ari. Maybe stop in Laith's shop and speak to him."

Lochlann groaned long and low. "Walking about town, huh? Well, maybe Elic could go with you. It will be a nice day for a walk," he said, his hands rubbing down his face to dig into his scruff.

"I would love to, darling," Elic started. "But I've got a big order to fill and should be on my way straight to the greenhouse." He kissed Ravena's cheek and then mine, leaving me confused. Or maybe he was confused. There was some definite confusion going on.

He turned in a swish of pale hair, leaving behind a mystery wrapped in an enigma.

"We'll see you at lunch, Ravena," Finn said, brushing his lips across hers and walking to the door.

"Yes. Lunch." Lochlann looked as confused as I felt but left anyway after placing a chaste kiss on Ravena's lips too.

Screw it, I thought, grabbing her up in a big hug and kissing her silly. She smiled against my lips, and I mentally congratulated myself as I left her.

"So we are all just going to be okay with her traipsing around town looking for Ari while dressed like a Faerie Princess? You can almost see her nipples through that dress. I mean, if you look just right, the outline is there," Lochlann said, looking over his shoulder at the house.

"Gods, no," Finn and I said at the same time, stopping to scowl at one another.

"I'll grab what I need from work and keep an eye on things," Finn said. "You two do whatever you have to and then ditch work when you can. We'll meet at the diner before lunch. If Ravena gets there early, Miri will keep an eye on her. I'll pay her if need be," he finished, looking stern. Finn never looked stern. I was still so confused.

"We need to buy some pants for her. Didn't she wear them more? What's with these dresses. Goddess, I wish Ari would come back. She would keep an eye on her without crushing her feeling of independence," I said, pinching the bridge of my nose.

We walked in silence for a bit.

"Do any of you know what is happening?" I asked.

No one answered.

Finn peeled off into the diner without further word; I assumed to talk to Miri. Lochlann and I walked, shuffling our feet toward our Queen and her orders.

# Chapter Thirty-One

## Lochlann

Rory had Unicorns to chase off, so I continued on with him until he entered the armory entrance, where I left him, surreptitiously circling back to the house. I ducked behind a tree as Ravena opened, then closed the door and started walking toward the town center.

Her face tilted up into the sun, and she smiled at everyone and everything that passed her. I smacked my forehead with my palm and trailed behind, close but not too close. She stopped and talked to Keena and her mates along the way. The girls' heads glued instantly together in serious conversation.

Keena's mates scanned their surroundings, and I gave them a little wave and put my finger to my lips when they spotted me. Their shoulders relaxed. We were all on high alert since the Trolls. The two men injured during the attack looked well, and the two that had been on the border with us when the attack happened looked ready to strike.

The Trolls had taken more than just Airmed, Teagan, and Arlie. Though Arlie was back, the sense of safety and freedom we once held had not returned and never would. Before the

Trolls, we never barred our doors at night or feared walking through the capital in the light of day. Now everything had changed.

Keena and Ravena parted with a hug, and Ravena continued on. Her complete disregard for her own safety was jarring. Where once she cowered in fear of every shadow, she made her way along with her head high and back straight. She was regal, stopping those she knew and talking to them, presumably about her missing friend.

As wonderful as it was to see her looking relaxed and at peace with her surroundings, it terrified me that she had so little thought for her own safety. She might need many more than four mates to protect her from the terrors in Talamh na Sithe. This was exhausting.

After one slow stroll through the markets and surrounding streets, she headed to Miri's to beat the lunch crowd. I darted through the alley, walking away from our little house to see if Finn was ready to leave his shop.

It was there that I saw Elic talking to a shadow that was tucked between buildings. He hadn't seen me yet, and I stopped, unsure of how to continue. I watched as he passed something into the shadow before turning to walk away.

When he looked over his shoulder, my eyes caught his, and he froze. Pulling the short sword, I sped to catch him. The shadow disappeared into the alley and was gone. "What are you doing, Elic? I thought you had to rush to the nursery?" I asked as I approached him.

"I took a moment. I paid one of the regulars a few coins to keep his eyes on Ravena since we were all working this morning," he laughed. The pitch was a little off, and his eyes a bit wide. "I didn't realize we would have the same idea."

"What patron?" I asked, fighting my instinct to put the sword at his throat. "Let us go inside and see this person."

"We can absolutely. I had hoped to keep my over protectiveness a secret. If we walk in there before lunch even starts, she will be on to us. I didn't want her to know I was worried. I trust her, but I don't trust Talamh na Sithe, and I hate to impinge upon her freedom."

And with that one statement, he had me. I didn't want to step on Ravena's freedom either. None of us did; she had opened up so much after Rowan died that I never wanted her to go back to that person she had been before. I didn't want to follow in the footsteps of my brother.

I would let her at least have the appearance of freedom, even if I watched from afar. We couldn't let her go completely independently; the land was wild and unsafe for strong females, let alone a delicate one.

If Airmed could be taken against her will, then anything can happen in Talamh na Sithe, for she was the strongest of us all. I wouldn't lose Ravena, and if that meant I had to be stealthy to not step on her toes, then that is what I would do.

Finn had already talked to Miri, and if we went in the minute her shift started, she would feel like we didn't trust her, and that would not be fair. Whether Elic was telling the truth or not, he was right. Something just didn't sit well with me, and maybe it was me being the annoying brother, I worried. We were so used to only relying on one another that it was hard to let an outsider in.

Ravena genuinely seemed to care for the little silver-haired Faeman with yellow eyes, so maybe I was overreacting. Whether or not they mated was beside the point; she should have all the friends she wanted. I just wanted to make sure they deserved her friendship. I stepped away from him and sheathed my short sword.

"You're right. I'm going to go get Finn. We had already planned on lunching here today; you're welcome to join us," I said, watching the other man. His shoulders relaxed, and his hands unclenched.

"Thank you for the invitation, but I must get back to the greenhouse. The Queen has ordered a hundred centerpieces for some function, and I must finish them. I only stepped away to check on Ravena and find someone unassuming to keep an eye on her. I should have known you brothers would already have a plan," he laughed, tossing his hair over his shoulder. "You seem very fond of her if nothing else. All of you."

"We are fond: fond and protective. She deserves everything we have to offer. The same goes for you." I watched as his face scrunched and his nose wrinkled.

"And she'll have it," he said, turning on his heel to leave. I followed behind him, continuing on my way to Finn's glass shop.

Elic walked straight to the nursery, never looking right nor left. What man does that? Maybe he needed protection too, that or he was so assured of his safety that he never felt the need to notice his surroundings. I had to wonder which of those it was. He gave a small wave when he opened his door. I walked the last several hundred lengths to pick up Finn.

He was putting tools and pieces away as I walked in, probably in preparation to go to lunch. In his arms, he had a large square parcel wrapped in brown paper.

"You finished it?" I asked, opening the door for him.

"I did. Help me hang it before lunch? It should be a simple matter of sliding the old window glass out and putting this one in." We smiled as we walked back towards the house. I hated to ruin his moment, but I told him about my run-in with Elic and watched as worry slipped across the lines of his face.

"I just don't know where he falls in all of this, if I'm being honest, and I don't have the talent to lie," he said. "The

Queen's guards watching us, and now this? It could be anything, and it could be nothing. It could be that we are being watched to see if there is duplicity among us. Maybe they are on to the ruse and know Elic and Ravena will never be mated. It could be anything. Maybe we are just paranoid," he finished, rubbing one hand on his pants as if to dry his palm. Shifting the parcel to the other, he repeated the process.

"I don't know," I said with a heavy sigh.

"Perhaps we are paranoid," he said again, slanting his blue eyes to mine.

"I feel like paranoia, in our case, is justified. Too many unusual things have happened since Rowan's happy, accidental death. Bless his weak heart." I chuckled.

"Indeed, I call dibs on Ravena tonight," he said, shoulder bumping me and making some weird, trilling noise in his throat.

"Dibs? What is dibs? I think not. I think I will call this dibs. I want to do the dibs with her." As the baby, he was always up on the latest slang. I wanted to trip him and run, but he carried the precious window he had worked so hard on. Then again, his magic was unbreakable glass, so I did it anyway and sprinted towards the house, chased by the sound of his curses.

We hung the window, then fought and elbowed one another until we were through the diner door where we straightened up, like two kids caught by their mother.

Ravena eyed us, then smiled when she took in our grinning faces, realizing we were up to no good. She still wore the damn dress but had tied an apron over it, which managed to hide the parts of her we wanted no one else to see. The black of her hair and the blue of her eyes contrasted stunningly against the pale of her dress and the deep red of her apron. It was as if she planned the outfit, and maybe she did.

"Gentlemen, here are your menus. I personally helped with the back strap of golden ram, so you should order that," she said, dropping her hand to my shoulder.

"While I am sure that the ram is amazing, I have been thinking about the turtle soup all day. Perhaps I will have the ram for dinner, though," I added when her face crumpled and her little nose scrunched.

"I will have the ram, Ravena," Finn said, winking at me. Cheeky fucker was trying to call the dibs, whatever that was. I hoped he choked on his ram.

"I will have an appetizer of the soup and the ram as well; I'm quite famished," I said, giving her my biggest smile.

Her own smile wrapped to her ears, and she dipped her head before walking away. She came back with drinks of chilled and sweetened tea, placing salads in front of us while we waited for the main course.

We watched with rapt attention as she flowed around the room with such grace and ease. She had a talent for this job.

People smiled at her and laughed here and there at her bad jokes. The mood of the place was light, and no one treated her in such a way to give us cause to worry. Maybe it was our presence, but Ravena had a gift with people, and no one got the wrong idea. I thought then that perhaps she had just as wide a range of magic as her friend Ari, only it was more subtle and less fireball-ish.

Ravena laid our meal with a swish of her skirts and a touch across the back of my neck that brought shivers down my spine. I was having dibs. That hair with that dress was giving me ideas. I sucked down my turtle soup and watched as she worked the crowd. As Fae paid their bills and left, they left her coins for her excellent service. She would make a lot of extra money if today was a typical day.

Finn was just about to cut into his back strap when Rory walked in. His dark scowl lightened when he saw Ravena just as mine had. Then he turned and gave the entire room a look that would kill. He had rainbow-colored hoof marks on his uniform, and I chuckled. He had gotten himself kicked by one of the impish bastards. Rainbow fluid had dried on his pant legs, and I laughed harder than I had in days. Rainbow smears on his face told me that his day had not gone as planned. Finn dropped his fork and nearly choked as he did the slow head-to-toe perusal of his brother, taking him in.

Ravena's hand went to her mouth to cover the sight of her jaw dropping, and her eyebrows flew to her hairline. She turned and grabbed a glass of sweetened and iced tea for him to hide her immediate reaction before meeting him at our table and handing him the glass.

"Can I interest you in the ram?" she asked, schooling her features into bland disinterest in his appearance. "I helped make it," she added in an attempt to entice him.

He looked at Finn and my plate, smirking at us through his rainbow-colored lashes. "I'll have what they are having." He raised an eyebrow at me in challenge, running a hand through his glittery, rainbow streaked hair in a pitiful attempt to straighten it.

I cut into the tender meat and moaned over the first bite. My eyes fell closed of their own accord, faking it at first before I noticed it wasn't bad. It was actually delicious. I dug in, and Finn got brave and followed suit. The table quieted as we shoveled food down our throats, wondering just how much input Ravena had in the making of it. She may be great with people and plants but had never shown that much skill with food. Maybe there was hope after all.

# Chapter Thirty-Two

## Ravena

I watched as they shoved bite after bite of the flame-cooked back strap. They seemed to like it very much. I hadn't lied, not exactly; I had helped make it. Miri had me cut the stag into thick slices and showed me how to use her ready made spice mix to cover both sides of it using butter to anchor it on. Then she placed it on a large wood-fired grill and cooked it to perfection, explaining each of the spices and how they worked together to bring out the meat's flavor.

I knew the brothers loved my cooking, but I might try some of the techniques that she used as they seemed to enjoy it too. Their eyes rolled back into their heads, and they dipped their bread in the juices on their plates until it was all gone. I refreshed their tea and carried away dirty plates.

They sat for a long time after they were done, nibbling at peach pie and talking about their respective days. They fit so well together, and my heart warmed at the sight of them.

When I would look over and find them glancing my way, my stomach tingled a little. I couldn't believe the change in them. They were having fun and playing with one another, sometimes like children. It was both heartbreaking and heart-mending at the same time. They were getting better. Though they still had nightmares and fought demons I would never understand, they were healing. It was a good thing.

I cleaned dishes and helped Miri recover as the lunch crowd faded into emptiness. Still, the brothers sat, finishing their pie and their drinks as they talked and laughed. It was nice to see.

"You did very well today, Ravena," Miri said, stretching her back out. "You are relieved of duty. I made you plates of the leftovers for dinner. Now now," she put her finger up when I started to interrupt her. "Those brothers look like they have plans for you that don't involve cooking." She gave me a naughty wink and a knowing smile. "Come back tomorrow, and I will show you my secret family poultry recipe." She shooed me out the door of the kitchen.

The men paid their bill, and I refused to take the coins they offered me for my service. I practically skipped with happiness home.

When I opened the door and saw the beautiful stained glass in the kitchen window, I almost cried. My hand flew to my mouth, covering my shock. Where once the plain glass had looked out into the garden, now a delicate hummingbird, done in blue and yellow glass, shimmered in the light of the afternoon sun.

The bird hovered over an intricate white rose with a leafy green vine woven around it. I had never seen anything more beautiful. I would no longer be able to see out into the garden, but it didn't matter. The bird was breathtaking, and I was speechless.

"Finn, there are no words," I said, turning to him and pulling him to me in a tight hug. "It's gorgeous."

"I'm glad you like it. I intended it to be a gift to you long ago, but the vision of it finished wasn't clear until recently." He cupped my face and kissed me, dipping his tongue to mine.

"Dibs," he said over his shoulder with a smug wink at Lochlann. Rory and I frowned at him, unsure what he meant.

Lochlann punched his arm hard enough to bruise and scowled as he walked to the door and out into the garden to stoke the fires that heated our water. Soon we would let the fires burn out and enjoy cool showers as the Talamh na Sithe summer heat would become suffocating.

Rory scowled his way into the bath, and I finally allowed myself to laugh at his condition. Yes, unicorns were dangerous. Yes, they could be deadly, but seeing him covered head to toe in unicorn cast-off had me laughing so hard I struggled to cover it.

"I hear you, Ravena," he said, shutting the door to the washroom behind him, the sound of his own laughter echoing in the closed space.

I changed into soft pants and a loose shirt before going out to touch the plants in our garden and pick the vegetables and fruit that had ripened. Finn found me first, settling on the bench with a book in his hand. He sat as I worked, the silence between us comfortable.

The others soon joined us. Rory, now bathed and clean, pulled a knife from his pocket and began to carve something out of a piece of wood. Lochlann walked the fence line, fixing anything he found amiss. We said nothing, each caught in their own thoughts. It surprised me how far he had come in such little time. The brothers' faces were relaxed, and their smiles light when their glances would flit to me from time to time.

I pulled vegetables and fruits off the plants I grew to take to Miri tomorrow so that she could work them into her recipes.

The afternoon stretched into evening, and we ate the dinner that Miri sent us home with. Their eyes closed with satisfaction as they ate, and I wondered which spice Miri had used to elicit that reaction. I would ask her tomorrow what she did to the meat.

Rory's eyebrows began to sink in upon themselves as the darkness grew. Elic had yet to come home from work, and he was worried, I could tell. Darkness brought wild creatures, and, even here in town, things weren't always safe. Especially recently.

A pang of sorrow struck my gut at the thought of Ari. She would come home. I knew that in my soul. I would miss her, but I could not allow myself to mourn her.

Elic said he had a big flower order to fill for the Queen, and I expected him much later than when he actually arrived. He strolled through the door, dirty and disheveled, just as I put my own book down on the couch and moved to disentangle myself from the brothers to get ready for bed.

"What a day," he said as he moved into the space. "Ten more centerpieces and I'm done." He blew out his breath, pushing his downy hair out of his eyes.

"I can help you in the morning if you want," I said, pulling my ankle out from under someone so I could stand.

"That would be great, Ravena." he came over, offering me a hand to steady myself so that I could get all four limbs free and stand on my own.

"Dinner is in the kitchen," Lochlann chimed in, watching Elic with a thoughtful gaze. As well as he seemed to be settling in, I would catch Finn and Lochlann, giving him odd glances from time to time. I wasn't sure what it all meant, and there was history there that I did not know, but I hoped that it would sort itself out.

"Those are the best words I've heard all day. I'm starved. Did you cook, Ravena?" he asked, giving me a sideways glance.

"No, not today. Miri was kind enough to send us home with dinner after my shift.

"Well then, okay, but sometime I want to try the cooking the brothers rave about all the time." He walked into the kitchen with a swish of his hips and wink over his shoulder. Behind him, Finn coughed, and Rory groaned so low it came out as a growl.

"I guess I have let my household duties go a bit since I've started working. I'll make a nice rabbit stew tomorrow." I went into the washroom to clean up and change for bed, smiling at the happy groans the brothers made at my dinner plans.

I lit candles in my room and slipped into a light-colored shift made from the silk of the fanged butterflies the Queen doesn't want in her gardens. It was the softest fabric I have ever felt. Rory bought it for me ages ago, but I had never worn it. Thin straps held the small slip of fabric in place, and it draped my breasts and deliciously hugged my hips.

Smiling in anticipation, I took the hummingbird pin out of my hair, combed my tangled locks with my fingers, then took the silver bodied hairbrush Lochlann and given me and brushed it straight again.

A low whistle sounded from the door. I turned to find Elic there staring at me. I gave him a shy smile.

"You look stunning," he said, coming in and taking the brush. Moving behind me, he separated my hair into sections and brushed it before braiding it in a loose, intricate four-stranded braid that went down my back. "There. Who is the lucky man tonight?" he asked, sitting on the edge of my bed.

"Oh, I don't know. Maybe no man," I laughed. "I never really know. It's an open invitation; we don't plan these things." I went to my dressing table and snuck a little lip stain on. I loved how the red made my blue eyes look so much sharper. 'It just works out." I gave him a soft smile. "You didn't change your mind, did you?"

"Goddess, no. I was just curious. I never saw you until after, well, Rowan died. I just wondered how you worked everything out." He laughed and gave a little shudder.

"Things are different now. We don't make choices for each other or plan anything." I stopped myself from saying more. I felt like I could trust him, but I stopped anyway.

"I know that things were bad with him. With Rowan. I know that the brothers had trouble with him for a long time, but you," he stopped. "Are you okay?" he asked, watching my reflection in the mirror.

I kept my face blank. "Yes, of course. We had all just settled in and started getting comfortable with one another. His death was a shock. There's been some adjustment, but time has smoothed things already, and we must move on." The omission flowed like honey from my tongue.

I'm not sure why I said it, except maybe I hoped that if I forgot about what happened, I could make it not real. You see, fate is a wheel that always turns. Rowan deserved what he got, but what about me? When the wheel came round again, would I pay the price for taking his life, or would fate see me as her tool and turn a blind eye to my actions? What of Ari? I worried over it for weeks afterward until I threw my hands up and decided I did what had to be done. Fate would judge me. The Goddess would judge me. I would not judge myself.

"I'm sure it was a shock. I just," Elic started. "I know Rowan was abusive to the brothers. It's hard for me to believe that he wasn't to you as well." He stopped talking and watched my face slide through my feelings.

I forced my shoulders to ease and my face to give a small smile. "Maybe I hadn't been here long enough. He wasn't kind, but it wasn't horrible. Why are you asking about this?" I turned from the mirror and leaned against my dressing table so he could not see my face as omissions slipped down the slope into the territory of lies.

"I have a friend who is being horribly abused by his lover. I just thought, like everyone else, that maybe Ari had made something for Rowan and that I could get some for my friend." His watery smile fell from his face, and I thought I saw a tear; he dropped his eyes from mine and gave a small sniffle.

"Ari is an amazing chemist, but she makes healing potions and women's medicines. She is trying to help us all conceive children. I have never seen her make poison or anything that would do harm. Perhaps when she gets back, you can speak with her about it, but as her best friend, I have not seen such a thing." I turned from him and found Lochlann standing in the door, staring at both of us. His bare, muscled chest was striking and shadowed in the light of the torches. He made my heart seize.

"Ravena," he said. "You take my breath. Perhaps I can pry you from Elic and have a moment.

"Of course," Elic rose and walked to me, giving me a little hug. "Have fun, sunshine," he said as he left.

Lochlann came to me, dropping his hands to my shoulders, and let them trace down my arms and fall to my sides where they rested on the small of my waist. "Finn says he has dibs. I don't exactly know what that means, and since I'm here and he's not," he trailed off and crushed his mouth to mine as he pulled me to him. "This is a beautiful nightshirt, but I'm afraid it will get wrinkled if you sleep in it." Taking my shift, he pulled it over my head, tossing it into a corner.

"Is that so?" I said, smiling up at him. There was no fire in my room yet, and the chilly night air pebbled my nipples.

"Yes," he said, bending to retake my mouth.

I laced my arms around his neck and kissed him back, keeping my light blue eyes pinned to his dark ones. "And as lovely as this braid is, I want to feel your hair slide across my skin." He tugged the ribbon, holding my hair, and wove his fingers through it until the long strands brushed my waist.

He pushed back, pulling the string on his pants and pushing them to the floor. I ran my hands over the sharp planes of his chest, tilting my mouth up to his for a kiss. The hardness of him pressed against my belly, making me groan. I slid my hand between us to grip him. He sighed into my mouth, and I took his pleasure into me, making it my own.

"I had dibs, Lochlann," Finn said from the doorway with a low chuckle. He leaned against the door frame with his arms crossed and a merry glint in his eyes. The fall of his bangs obscuring one of them.

"Finders keepers." Lochlann pulled me tight, crushing my breasts against him. He took my lips and found my tongue, causing heat to drive through to the core of me like an arrow.

I felt my hair moved to the side and warm lips trace down my neck. I moaned, resting my back against Finn. I felt Rory's absence, and I wanted him to suck my nipples. I wanted them all. We had never been together, all four, and if Elic hadn't been new to our home, I would have called to Rory.

Fingers traced my spine up and down, bringing goosebumps to my arms. Tilting my head, I gave Finn my neck, and he bit into it, causing just enough pain to shoot straight to my core and make my knees weak.

Lochlann pulled me onto the bed and placed my knees on either side of his ears while Finn guided his cock to my lips, thrusting in eagerness, making me take him all. The salty-sweet taste of him hit my tongue, and I ground against Lochlann's mouth as he licked across me, making my legs shake and my vision dim.

Finn worked my mouth fast, touching the back of my throat with his tip before pulling out and doing it again. He gripped the back of my head and kept his pace brisk until he shuddered and withdrew from me. Fisting his cock, he shot hot fluid down my chest and belly and crushed his lips to mine. Lochlann's arms anchored on my hips and held me tight to him while he fucked me with his lips and tongue. I came screaming, out of control, and thrusting my hips onto his face. I collapsed into Finn's arms, and he flipped me onto my back before thrusting into me.

I was so wet that he met no resistance. He glided in and out with slow, measured strokes. His eyes never leaving my face that was caged between his arms. I felt every contour of him as my muscles tightened. The stony ridge of him driving me wild. He leaned up, and I looked between us, his come still glistened on my breasts, and I could see his glistening cock pull out and bury deep within me once again. I watched as he fucked me, each thrust of his hips bringing me closer. I tilted up to him, changing the angle, and felt it start deep in my core.

I learned a lot about orgasms in sex class, but I had never had one of my own until Rowan was gone. The class talked about orgasms clinically. Touch this spot to achieve that result. There is nothing clinical about an orgasm. They can be hard and deep within your body or sharp and rolling just at your core. No orgasm is the same, and they are all magical.

This one hit me so deep that I felt my entire uterus throb with it. Animal noises escaped my lips, and my heart pounded into my ears. Finn came again once my muscles locked down on him, clenching him over and over. His cry was surprised and loud. His forehead dropped to mine as we both fought to catch our breaths, chests heaving one against the other.

He dropped to my side and was replaced immediately between my thighs by Lochlann. I wasn't sure I could take it. My body lay limp and spread like a fallen star under him, and I could barely keep from being smashed into the bed, let alone move with him. Then his lips found mine, and his body stilled within me. I breathed in the scent of lightning and love that rolled off of him, and my body woke up and wrapped around his. Lochlann flipped us.

Laying on his back next to his brother, he settled me on his hips, pushing so deep inside of me that it ached where he touched. I rose over him and slid back down his soaking wet body. He reached up, pinching my nipples, and I felt the heaviness build in my core again. Finn watched through lidded eyes as I rode Lochlann.

I ground against him over and over until I felt another orgasm build. I chased it with my hips, sliding up and over and then back and forth. I chased it until it ripped out of me with a guttural groan and clenching muscles.

Lochlann closed his eyes, gripped my hips, and pounded into me, releasing as deep as he could, bathing my womb with his life. His hands dropped to his side, and his face went slack. As Finn pulled me down to nestle between them, I caught a glimpse of silver hair from my open doorway. When I raised my head to look, all I saw was darkness.

## Chapter Thirty-Three

## Finn

"That was the most beautiful thing I have ever seen, Ravena," I said as she snuggled into me, pressed between my brother and me. I missed Rory at that moment. Where we would put him, I didn't know, but I missed him all the same.

Unable to leave Ravena in the soup we had made of her, I rose despite her protests to get a warm wet rag to wipe her off with. She hummed in appreciation at the feel of the warmth between her legs.

"Thank you," she whispered from behind closed eyes. I tossed the rag in the corner and skipped lighting the fire. We would keep each other warm.

"You're welcome, love," I whispered in her ear with a kiss on her cheek.

She smiled, half-asleep already. Her black hair formed a pillow on which my brother slept, and her pale blue skin shimmered slightly in the darkness. I had never seen her do that before. She almost glowed, and it took my breath. She nearly vibrated with happiness, and a sense of peace so deep settled over me that it was almost uncomfortable.

I traced the lines of her face with the tips of my fingers and realized something. I loved her. Goddess, I loved her. She had saved our lives in so many ways. Her will to forgive and inability to hate us for what we had done to her had saved our souls. She had killed to save us. Never had I loved anything more. Not ever.

Then I freaked out. I started shaking against her, and she pulled herself against me.

"Shhhhhh," she said in her sleep. "No nightmares tonight, my love," she said, her voice heavy with sleep.

I stilled at her words. She never used any term of endearment with us. Not ever. I began to tremble again.

Only it wasn't nightmares that made me shake; it was hope. Hope, dreams, and plans for a future where we all found happiness scared me more than anything else could. I knew fear. I understood it. This was something else. I pulled Ravena so tightly to me that her breath snuffled against my chest. Sighing, I fell asleep with her in my arms and thoughts of love in my head.

I heard screaming before the sun split the horizon. I rolled over, confused by the noise. Ravena was up and down the hall before I could put together that Rory was having another nightmare. She knew without being fully awake to grasp it; she just knew. Down the hall, her little feet pattered. She took no sheet, and her wild hair flowed behind her like darkness.

I rose slowly to follow, my mind muddled and foggy. I followed the sound of Ravena's whisper soft voice and found her wrapped around Rory, soothing him. His eyes were closed, his breathing steady, and the screams had stopped. The light of his hearth fire glistened on the sweat clinging to his skin. His breathing shuddered once and then evened out again.

Ravena ran her hands through his shaggy black hair and down his back in steady strokes. Leaning out, I found the door to Elic's room closed and no flicker from his hearth visible, and I wondered where he was. We rarely closed doors, and it was odd to see it shut. When I went to open it, I found his room empty and his bed mussed. Dread settled deep into my heart. I knew something wasn't right; I just didn't know what.

Lochlann stumbled by me, giving me a shoulder bump on his way into Rory's room. He dropped down behind Ravena and pulled her to him, his eyes unseeing. He just knew she had left him and had stumbled along behind her without question.

After a quick check of the house to prove that Elic was not there, I climbed into bed with my brothers and our mate. I slipped behind Rory and sandwiched him between Ravena and myself as he was less inclined to freak out about having a man behind him than Lochlann was.

In no time, we were asleep again. Rory had no more nightmares, and nothing disturbed us until dawn cracked the night sky, lightening the room and awakening us. Ravena claimed one washroom, and we shared the other to rinse off and get ready for the day.

When we came into the kitchen, we found plates of steaming hot food greeting us. Elic was dressed and wearing Ravena's apron. Hot tea was poured and sitting on the table. "Elic, you shouldn't have," Ravena said, hugging him to her. He was a few hairs shorter than she, and his silver hair contrasted wildly with her black.

He hugged her hard. "I told you, cooking is part of my magic, you help with plants, and I'll help with cooking. It's the least I can do," he said, brushing her hair back from her face and kissing her cheek. "You're surely not leaving the house with your hair like that, are you?" he laughed and swatted at her shoulder.

I watched as Ravena's eyes lit up at his antics, and I worried anew. I didn't trust him. I didn't even like him, but she clearly did. "Where were you last night?" I asked.

"What do you mean?" he answered, giving me a wicked case of side-eye.

"Rory had a nightmare, and I looked for you. You weren't here," I said.

I felt the room go still around me.

"Did you check the new washroom?" he answered, twisting his hair around a finger and letting it go.

"I did not." The little man's shoulders relaxed.

"After Rory and I, well. I took a bath and fell asleep there for a bit, I guess. The water was cold when I woke up. I didn't know Rory needed me. I must have slept through it."

"That's all right," Rory said, tussling his hair. "Ravena to the rescue." He winked at her and kissed her lightly on the cheek. "I don't remember any of it. I just woke up with a bunch of hairy arms and legs all over the place and one sticky-sweet female plastered to my back." he laughed, tossing his head back.

And just like that, it was over. We all grabbed plates and stuffed ourselves on Elic's cooking. It was good. Maybe even magical if eggs, cured pork, porridge, and toasted bread can be magical. We stuffed ourselves, leaving nothing for the alley rats.

We cleaned the kitchen together as the sky grew brighter. Ravena stopped by the window out to the garden, a surprised gasp coming from her. Rory was at her side in an instant, and together, they opened the door, tripping over each other to get outside. We followed, unsure of what had driven them outdoors.

Above us, the sky undulated in lavender and pink waves. The rising sun did nothing to chase away the deep and colorful sky. I had never seen anything like it. I felt magic kissing along my skin; it made my hair stand on end. Ravena's eyes went impossibly wide, and her hand shot to her mouth.

"The Goddess," Lochlann whispered.

You could see trails of magic and power, and it was as if the entire capital had screeched to a halt. At that moment, the world stopped moving and was still under our feet. Never- ever had I felt anything so powerful.

"Airmed," Ravena said as tears poured down her face. "Ari." She dropped to her knees and started sobbing. "I feel her. She's home."

Elic's head snapped back like he'd been slapped. He turned and caught me watching him, my eyes narrowed upon his, and I was back to not trusting him, magical breakfasts aside.

"I hope what you say is true, but please don't get your hopes up, little bird," I dropped to my knees beside her, cradling her in my arms.

The feeling of magic slipped through the air and was gone. The Goddess's sky faded to the blue of Ravena's eyes, and the moment passed.

We rose and came back inside to get ready for the day. Elic went into his room to change and headed out to wherever he was going. I met Lochlann's eyes, and he nodded once in understanding, following Elic out the door. Rory had taken my place and wrapped Ravena in his arms and was rocking her side to side, kissing her hair.

Until this morning, I had no real plans for the day. Having finished the house project, I intended to stay with Ravena until she went to the diner for lunch, but that had changed. Elic was up to something, and I wanted to keep an eye on him until I figured out what it was.

"I'm going to pop into the shop for a bit. There are a few orders to fill before we get to our days of rest." I went to Rory and Ravena and wrapped them both in my arms. "I'll see you at lunch, Ravena." I kissed the top of her hair before pulling away. "Brother, a word?"

He followed me to the door; I stepped through, pulling him behind me and shut the door. "Stay with her, Rory. Please. Something isn't right, and it doesn't feel safe to leave her." I gripped his forearm with mine and held his eyes.

"You're paranoid," he whispered, but I heard the edge of worry too.

"I hope that I am. You felt the magic too. I know you did. Keep her close. Surely you can miss one day of work. At least a few hours." I begged him, willing him to feel the unease that coursed through my veins.

Sighing, "I've missed many hours of work. If we don't want to draw the Queen's eye, I must go. We all must go. Fear from the Troll attack is dying down, and while it was reasonable to miss work during that time, it will be noticed now- for all of us. We need to keep to our schedule," he said. "I share your unease; I do. I never want to leave her, but for now, we must get back to normal, or we'll be noticed."

"There is no normal anymore. Not to those of us who protect The Eight. No doubt the other houses are putting their females first, surely the Queen understands." My need to follow Elic was so strong; I had to fight to stand still.

"I'll stay a bit, then take her to the diner. That's the best I can do," he said, and my heart sank. He was right. We couldn't be too careful with Ravena. Still, we also couldn't change our behavior too radically and draw attention to ourselves either.

"Okay," I said, taking a deep breath. "Okay." I hugged him to me and left him.

I knew Rory didn't share my reluctance to trust Elic and that Ravena was deeply enamored with him. I had never disliked Elic, not until now, but my instincts screamed at me to listen, and I would. After the incident with the Trolls, I would never ignore them again.

I ducked past Ari's darkened bakery and scanned the streets on the way through town. I found Lochlan at the fountain in the square, feeding pigeons bits of bread. I sat next to him, saying nothing.

"He's a quick little fuck," he said, not looking at me. I managed to follow him through Connaugh and lost him before the river.

"The river?" I asked, shocked.

A tumultuous, fast-moving river ran near the furthest reaches of the western border. It was a wild, empty place. Patrols did not go there because the vast stretch of land was uninhabited by any but the smallest lesser Fae creatures. The mountain range beyond formed our border with the next land and was impassable. Even birds did not cross those high peaks.

Connaugh was a small town between the capital and the river. Mostly soldiers lived there, and it was often considered part of the capital. Connaugh was little more than a shantytown filled with unpaired men living in squat homes thrown together.

Despite the lack of women, most Fae chose to live with brothers, lovers, friends, or like-minded individuals. Few Fae chose to live alone, and those Fae lived in Connaugh. I never liked going there. Dark loneliness and old desperation was such a part of the inhabitants that it permeated the air.

Just because the Queen paid well didn't mean that all her soldiers could be helped by financial gain or even cared for such a thing. Many of the broken soldiers that lived there were Huntsman who failed to find their quarry or archers who had lost their magic. She used those Fae for any task too dark for those of us who still had hope, free will, and a conscience.

Why would Elic be going there? And if not there, then why would he be going to the river?

"I couldn't follow him and stay hidden. We need a Huntsman," he said, crushing the bag that held the pigeons' bread.

"They are likely all looking for Ari," I said, scrubbing my hand across my face.

"The search has been called off. Only Seal still hunts her, and word is he's gone mad."

"Fuck," I said, looking at the clear blue sky. Clouds formed on the horizon, and it looked like it might rain. We hadn't seen a good hard rain in many weeks, and it would be welcome for those who relied on it.

"I have a good relationship with Arias, one of Arlie's mates, and a Huntsman. I will ask him. I don't like this. I don't like any of this."

"I don't either. Let's go and be done with our day as quickly as we can so that we can get back to her. We will keep her safe, Lochlann." I stood, cracking my neck from side to side and willing myself to believe my own words.

"I hope so, I do." We parted ways, each deep in thought. I skirted the edges of town, looking for any signs of Elic, but there were none. His greenhouse was closed, and the shades drawn. It was early yet; I would come back later and see if he was around.

In my shop, I grabbed a few things I needed to work on and shoved them into bags. When Rowan lived, this place was a haven for me. I was expected to work and provide for the family, so I was never mistreated by him for coming here. In the end, though, I had almost lost my magic and refused to come. Rowan had that effect. Lately, I saw this place as a distraction.

I did not need the space. I only needed a few tools, materials, and my magic to create what I sold. Not for the first time did I think about moving my operations closer to home or even to it. I could take space in the garden and build a small shed, then rent a booth in the marketplace, which was within eyesight of our house.

Feeling better now that I had a plan, I walked back and found the greenhouse doors still locked. Some hours had passed, and the place should be open. The feeling of unease grew stronger within my gut, and I headed home to verify that Ravena was, indeed, okay. Rory was a big boy, and I worried not for him, not really. We had survived the worst that could be done to us. Rory's broken heart aside, I didn't care if Elic was sleeping with others. He had signed no contract and taken no vows, but if whatever he was doing harmed Ravena in any way, I would kill him myself.

# Chapter Thirty-Four

## Lochlann

"Arias, please," I asked the other man. "I understand that this puts you in a difficult position, but we need your help. My greatest fear is that we have brought a dangerous person into our home that will cause harm to Ravena. Put yourself in our shoes," I finished, dropping onto the bench outside the armory.

"You mean that the Queen has sent someone into your home that you fear may harm your family," he said, turning his sharp eyes to mine.

"We asked for him," I said, omitting the reasons as to why.

"That's a fine line. Word is another had been chosen anyway." He picked at a loose thread on his doeskin pants.

"Be that as it may, will you help us or not? We need to find him, maybe follow him a little. We just need answers," I implored. There were others I could go to, but I knew Arias better and trusted him. Even if he did not help, he would not spread the word that we were seeking it.

"What if the answer leads back to the crown. I don't want to cause trouble for my family." He would not meet my eyes, and I worried he would say no.

"Just walk with me through town. We are friends. That would not be unusual. Whatever we find, we find. No one will be the wiser. Hopefully, we find nothing. Perhaps Elic is in a relationship with someone else, and that is fine too. The family will deal with that hurt, but if he is doing something nefarious that could lead to physical harm, I need to know. Something isn't right. Ravena is taken with him and trusts whatever he does or says. What if he leads her into danger, and she is killed? I will kill him with my bare hands and draw the Queen's undivided attention before I allow that to happen. Please, if it were Arlie, you would want to know. Please help us," I finished.

Sighing, he rose. "Let's walk then. Did you bring something of his?"

I handed him a black ribbon that Elic tied his hair with a day or two ago. Closing his eyes, he pressed it between his fingers. Handing the ribbon back to me, we began to walk. We followed a rabbit's trail through the town, to our house, and back through the town again. Any bird watching from the sky would have thought us mad as there was no rhyme or reason to our path.

The more we walked, the more agitated Arias became. "He is doing this on purpose," he said. "His trail is filled with thoughts of deceit. He isn't frantic; he's simply evading. These circles are intentional."

We walked through Connaugh and stopped at the river. Then we walked back. Arias became more agitated, and I realized how much a Huntsman's magic made them suffer. Once accepting a task, they could not quit. No wonder Seal was rumored to be mad right now. No wonder Connaugh was filled with broken Huntsmen.

When we came back into the capital proper, Arias took a sharp turn and walked straight to the Greenhouse. Elic stood pale and disheveled in the back of the place, whispering to a customer. When he looked up and saw us standing there, his eyes widened. Arias walked into the greenhouse and visibly relaxed, the need to hunt gone from him.

"Get your answers; let me know if you need any further help. Something tells me you'll need it. I'll be there if you do," he said, picking up a lovely pink flower close to the door and walking to the back. He handed Elic some gold.

"You were right, Lochlann. This is the perfect plant for an angry wife. Thanks for bringing me." And with that, he covered our tracks and gave Elic an explanation as to why I was with the Huntsman.

"Anytime, Arias," I chuckled, feigning amusement. "Happy mate, life is great!"

"No kidding. Hopefully, this will get me off of the couch." He winked and was gone.

Elic visibly settled, his face smoothing out into smirking, overconfident pleasantness.

"Elic," I greeted the other man. "We came by earlier, and you seemed to be late opening. I hope all is well," I said, walking through the plants like I didn't have a care in the world. "I think Ravena would like this one, don't you?" I asked, picking up plants and putting them down.

"I think she would. The blue of the flower almost matches her skin," he said, walking to me. "I had an early meeting with the Queen regarding her centerpieces. She wanted some rare flower that only grows near the river. I've been all over Talamh na Sithe to try to fill this order. Come. Look at them. Tell me what you think." He walked away, leading me deeper into the greenhouse. Warily, I followed.

On the back table sat a huge display of flowers set into golden bowls, each larger than the next. The bowls were arranged in tiers and looked like fountains filled with colorful blooms instead of water. The top bowl was crowned with the most exotic flower I have ever seen; the petals changed color like the beat of a heart. From blue to green, then yellow to red, it changed. No color was left out, and the effect was stunning. I had never seen anything like it.

Maybe Elic was telling the truth, and my paranoia was getting the better of me.

"I've never seen anything like it," I said, meaning the compliment. "Lovely."

"Yes, but I'll be glad when this ball or whatever is over so that I can find some peace." He stifled a loud groan and stretched his back. "Take the plant; she'll love it." He gave me a wink.

I stood undecided between questioning him further and keeping my thoughts to myself. I chose the latter and walked away.

I checked at the armory and received my assignment for the day. As much as I laughed at Rory over the unicorns, I had to laugh at myself now. My assignment was to excavate and move a clan of Luisne Badgers, making a nuisance of themselves under the homes of the oldest and most powerful Fae living near the palace.

Personally, I think they are cute little bastards with their wriggly noses and plucky attitudes. They also glowed at night and were downright adorable, even when they snarled at you and tried to take your arms off with their teeth, but the snooty old Fae across town wanted them off of their lawns. Sighing, I grabbed some traps and went to catch badgers.

Hours later, when I returned tired and stinking from being sprayed multiple times by the Luisnes, I also glowed as I was covered in their goo. I had lost my appreciation for their plucky attitudes. Still, I had succeeded in relocating them to the

Anthril Forrest, where they belonged. What a day, but during my day of catching badgers, I had thought long and hard about Elic and his possible deception.

In the end, I believed it was a deception. Arias had felt it, and so did I. Yes, he had a large order to fill for the Queen, and he certainly got the Tuarceatha flower from the river, but something did not feel right. I would get to the bottom of what was going on with him, and if he was doing anything that would hurt Ravena or jeopardize her place in our home, I would kill him myself.

## Chapter Thirty-Five

## Rory

I watched Ravena from the chaise. She hummed as she worked in the kitchen. After dropping her off at Miri's, I had gone to work as usual despite my brother's misgivings and had come home to find her cooking.

Miri had sent herbed chicken but had left Ravena in charge of the side dishes, and fear clawed at me as I watched her bake some sort of potato dish in the oven. She cut lettuce for a salad and arranged everything artfully on the table.

As my brothers trickled in, they froze at the sight of her and not because she was beautiful, which she is, but because she was cooking, which she was. I sighed, regarding Lochlann over the edge of my book, letting him know with my eyes that he should run.

I took in the fact that he glowed and stunk like a Luisne Badger and chuckled. Maybe running wasn't an option for him since he'd glow like a comet as he went.

Finn had begun setting up shop at home and was happily working in the garden to arrange a space. His plan to build on to the house and then sell his glass at the market was not a bad one. He was right that Talamh na Sithe had proven unsafe for our girl. One of us needed to stay close at all times to keep an eye on things. When Finn finalized his plans, we would help him build whatever he needed.

Lochlann went to the washroom to bathe, glowering and glowing, while Ravena covered her laughter with a dishtowel.

"You have the most interesting jobs. I will never reach the level of entertainment that you do," she said, sipping dark liquor from a short glass.

"What are you drinking, love?" I asked.

"Miri gave me a bottle of whiskey to go with our dinner; she thought I might need it. She put me in charge of making sides today, and then the counter they were on collapsed out of the blue, and she had to start over. It was a heck of a day." She tossed her head back, laughing. "Anyway, Miri tweaked my recipe and made them even better, so I'm trying the new version on my own."

"The counter just collapsed?" I asked, smiling to myself. Miri had finally learned we weren't kidding about Ravena's cooking.

"Yes. It was the oddest thing." She sipped her whiskey, eyes fixed on mine.

I rose and went to her, dropping a kiss on her lips. I hadn't spent much time with her since Elic came and need took me. I picked her up and sat her on the counter, my fingers dipping beneath her dress to find her core. I rubbed my thumb into her wetness and traced her with it. She dissolved into me, placing her head on my shoulder, and I realized how much I missed her.

Her little nub was stiff and swollen, and I strummed it until she cried out, her breath catching in my hair. She gripped me, and I wanted to sink into her, even though we were in the kitchen and our family was home.

I enjoyed Elic, and I enjoy men, but there is something about Ravena's heart and her soaking wet folds that I needed too. Her scent drove me mad, and the smell of her pleasure drifted between our bodies.

I picked her up and carried her to my room just as the front door shut and Elic walked in. Surprise crossed his face and then something else. We had talked about it, and he understood our position and how we all felt. At least he said he did. That look made me wonder. Then I heard his laugh and relaxed; he said something that made Finn chuckle.

Ignoring them, I eased Ravena's dress over her head and bent my head to her nipple. She arched against me and wove her fingers through my hair. Unable to wait, I lowered her to the bed and met her lips as I pushed into her. Goddess, she was so hot, and just the feel of her wetness soaking my balls had them tightening.

Needing to prolong it, I made myself pull out and dragged her to her knees before entering her from behind. She gasped at the feel of it, and I froze, worried about my roughness.

"No, Rory. I like it," she said, her arms trembling to hold her. Trusting her word, I started again, thinking that if I couldn't kiss her soft lips, I might last longer.

I was wrong.

I reached down and flicked my fingers across her, causing her back to bow. In minutes she clenched around me, coming with a sharp cry, and I pushed deep into her, bumping her womb with my head as I released my seed, tossing my head back with a strangled groan as I filled her.

Never had anything felt more delicious. Never. She would become an addiction I could never tire of. I knew it. I wanted to be in her for hours, but she tore the stamina from me with her body and had me coming in moments.

I needed to practice more.

I ran my hand down her bare back as the last convulsions left her. She sighed sweetly, her thighs working to hold her up. I pulled her hair into a bundle and kissed the back of her neck. "Thank you for giving me so much. Someday I swear I will make it last longer for you." I chuckled a little at my failings.

"There's no need to thank me, Rory, and the fact that you've left me unable to walk means you were brilliant," she said, her words muffled by my pillow.

I gave her ass a sharp little smack, thrilling at her happy squeak, and pulled out of her. The sight of my come dripping down her legs and onto my bed covers made me hard again, but the sight of Elic watching from the door changed that. He gave me a saucy smile and turned away to his room as unease rippled through my gut.

Somewhere along the way, things had changed between us. I still loved him, in truth, but I no longer trusted him blindly the way I once did. He seemed happy enough to share me and our life. Maybe it was just leftover fear from a time when we couldn't be together. I don't know, but something inside me rippled with fear.

I didn't think he would ever touch Ravena, not in that way, and I didn't want him to. I cared nothing for sharing her with my brothers, for we were family, but Elic was not family, and I was starting to see that.

Ravena brought him here for me, and now I wasn't sure I wanted to share my life with him. I knew Elic. I'd known him for many years, and I knew he wasn't this easy. I kept waiting for the fight to start or the drama to begin. That was Elic. As much as I loved his body and what it did to me, I knew him, and he wasn't acting like himself. As much as I had once needed him, things had changed.

I kissed Ravena again and left her on my bed to nap. She gave a long sigh when my lips caressed the soft curve of her ear. In the washroom, I wiped myself down and pulled my pants on. I heard Finn chuckle when he walked by Ravena, seemingly asleep, where she dropped.

"You have a way with her, Rory," he whispered outside the washroom door, his voice light and happy. It made me smile. I felt inadequate, especially when compared to my brothers. I had no idea how any of this was supposed to work and no frame of reference with a woman. Still, she wasn't faking being passed out in a heap, so I must be doing something partly right. That, or she is as clueless as I am.

Elic met me in the hall and led me back to his room, pushing his door closed behind me. He dropped to his knees and had my pants down and his mouth on my cock before I could register his actions.

"Now let me please you in the way you like," he said, tracing the lines of my limp cock with his tongue.

I let him. I did.

My soft cock hardened in his mouth. Putting my hand on his head, I watched as he bobbed up and down my length, playing with my balls and tracing my entrance with a wet finger. He slipped it inside and found that gland that brings so much pleasure.

He did know me. He knew everything I liked and was excellent at seeing to my pleasure, but it felt empty and forced.

Wrong even. Especially at this moment when I had just left Ravena. I should have stopped him, but I didn't.

His tongue licked the tops of my thighs and found my cock again. He inhaled deeply through his nose, and I wondered what he thought about the scent of my mate covering me. He said nothing, just bobbed faster, taking me down his throat until my head was deep within him. He held it there, and I felt my balls tighten. He pulled back, took a breath, and sucked my cock down his throat as he palmed his stiff shaft, working himself into an orgasm that he released across my feet. I came into him, and he swallowed it all. With me so deep inside of his throat that he barely had to try, I simply filled his belly.

He stayed on his knees, holding me as I rested my hands in his hair. I tilted my head back as my heart slowed and sighed. He felt good; Gods did he feel good.

Perhaps the problem was me, and I just needed to let go and settle in. Ravena knew why he was here and did not care. Maybe we could have it all, but perhaps too much had happened to go back to those days. Maybe I didn't want to go back.

I pulled him to me and kissed him lightly. Watching him smile at me and give me a knowing wink. "I know the plan is to breed her. I understand. I do, Rory. Don't worry about any of it. I'm here to be what you need while you are doing what you have to do." My brows knit together at his unkind words.

Hearing him talk about her like she was an animal angered me. I said nothing as he left the room, shutting the door to leave me alone.

After he was gone, my anger only grew. I cared for Ravena; she was not some beast here to breed. She was ours, and we were hers. It wasn't like he was suggesting. Not even a little bit, and that he even gave voice to his thoughts about her changed me. Something shifted.

Maybe my attraction to him had been due in part to Rowan's absolute refusal to allow our relationship. Forbidden fruit is always sweeter. Rowan almost killed me for loving him. Maybe I loved him as a small rebellion against the tyranny that was Rowan. Maybe that is what had changed me; it's hard to say.

I still cared, and he still brought me pleasure, but there was something else I couldn't put my finger on, which brought me back to Ravena. She was family now. She fit with my brothers and now with me like we had been made for her. And maybe we were. She had endured too much to allow anyone else to hurt her. Not even with words.

Perhaps Elic was a true friend and didn't grasp the situation fully yet. Perhaps we would settle into something better with him here, time would tell, but if his ways had not changed and if he brought any harm to Ravena, my love for him would not keep him safe from me. Not even a little bit.

# Chapter Thirty-Six

## Ravena

I awoke in Rory's bed. Rolling over, I found him asleep next to me. Night had fallen, and hearth fires burned, but no torches lit the space. I knew that it was late and that I had slept for many hours. Stretching, I felt the pull of dried drool on my face and semen on my legs. With a smile on my face, I rose, walking to the washroom to clean up.

I paused, looking back, and watched Rory sleep. His scarred face was relaxed and soft by the dim light of the fire. Something moved in me, and I went to him, brushing the hair from his brow and letting my fingers trace his jawline. The scars from many fists only made him more beautiful. Of all the men, he confused me the most.

He was a contradiction between hard and soft and the dichotomy between war and peace. Both raged within him, pushing and pulling so that neither won. He was a man always on the edge between dark and light. I felt sick to my stomach, but not in a bad way when I looked at him. I had never felt that before and wondered what it meant. Kissing his cheek, I went to bathe.

I had promised to help Elic with the last of the Queen's centerpieces. I should have done it sooner as the strain of the long week on his face was telling. Easing myself into the deep warm water with a sigh, I soaked. Minor aches and pains fled in the warmth of the water, and I lay for a while before I washed.

My life had turned into something truly remarkable. From the ashes of Rowan's funeral pyre, a beautiful plant had grown and continued to grow as it bloomed into something surreal. Like the vine in Finn's window, it wrapped around us, enfolding us into one being. One thing.

Peace and happiness filled me at the thought of Rory, Lochlann, Finn, and even Elic. I was surrounded by lovers and had found something different with them all. I was grateful.

When the water cooled, I stepped out, wrapping a dressing gown around me. In the kitchen, I put on a pot to boil for tea. Just as I leaned against the counter, I heard a soft knock on the back garden doors. Unsure, I went to see who might be here at such an odd time.

Ari's scowly mate stood, shadowed but unmistakable, by the light of the setting moon. I opened the door for him.

"Seal? What is it?" I tried to whisper and failed as I pulled him into the room.

"Ari is safe. I will say nothing else. She loves you, Ravena, and it is for your safety that you don't know what's going on," he said, looking at me with hard brown eyes.

"Seal. Please. I need to see her," I begged him, my voice breaking.

"I'm sorry, Ravena. It's impossible. She wanted me to give you this." He handed me a heavy bag, and I knew what it contained. Glass clinked as I took it.

"Tell her I love her," I said, a tear slipping down my face.

"She loves you. What is now will not be forever. That is her promise," he said, his eyes softening, and I saw in that short moment what Ari must see every day in him.

The depth of his love for her shown in his eyes. I nodded once and watched him slide through the door and melt into the night. He stopped at the fence, "A silver-haired man left your yard, moving with the shadows and trying to hide. I don't know who he is. Tell your mates and watch your back. No one is safe in this land." He was gone before I could ask a single question.

I took the bag of Ari's potions and went to my empty room, shutting the door behind me. I pulled the rug back and exposed the floor underneath. I picked up a loose floorboard, and one by one put an array of colored bottles into the hole in the floor alongside the few I already had from the bakery. I replaced the board and then the rug, resting on my hands and knees afterward.

Ari was safe, but Ari was gone. I understood, but I didn't. Tears slipped from my eyes. Why couldn't everything be good? Ari had trusted me with her potions, and I would see that The Eight who needed them got them. Make that seven. A whimper escaped me, and the tears fell harder.

Make that six.

Strong arms scooped me off the floor where I lay, and I was cradled to a large, hard chest.

"Tell me," Lochlann said. The scent of lightning and wild storms met my nose, causing me to relax.

I told him. It came pouring out with my tears until there were no more tears to cry. He held me on my bed, rocking me the way a mother might a child. He murmured into my hair that it would be okay and that I must trust Ari. He also cautioned against telling anyone what had happened. I understood his caution. Something had been in the air, and it was something enormous. Whatever magic covered Talamh na Sithe these last days would change the world.

When my sobs changed to sniffles and then stopped altogether, I pushed away from him.

"Thank you," I said, bringing my eyes to his. He smiled down at me, but it was not a smile of happiness.

"I love you, Ravena," he said.

A sharp intake of breath was all I could manage. He stood with me, like I weighed nothing, and took me into the bathroom. He wiped my face with a warm cloth, kissing my nose when he was done.

"What of the man?" I asked.

"Probably one of the Queen's guards checking on us. They've been doing it for a while now. We'll keep you safe, regardless. Let's dress, and I'll walk you to the greenhouse.

"Okay." My breath caught in my throat and roared in my ears. My heart pounded in my chest, and I felt panic rise. Steadying myself, I followed him to the kitchen to get tea and make breakfast.

Finn stood, a pan of hotcakes already cooking. His worry-filled eyes met mine. He folded me in his arms and inhaled my scent deeply. I sighed into him, the last of my anxiety shuddering out of me.

Rory padded into the kitchen not long after, taking in the scene, his head tilting sideways.

"Everything okay?" he asked.

"Yes. Fine," I said, pulling from Finn and going to Rory. I rose to my tiptoes and kissed his lips before taking my tea and going to dress.

Their whispers followed me, and I shut the door to my room, sinking into my bed.

Did I love them?

I loved Ari. I knew what that love felt like. I loved my sisters, but that was a different kind of love. I liked the men. They made my body sing and gave me things I never thought I'd have when I came here.

Love? Not yet, but someday. Someday the soft looks and tender feelings would transmute into love. I believed that. Maybe I was already there and couldn't accept it. I wouldn't rush myself or them. I also wouldn't cheapen the truth that I cared and cared deeply or attempt to lie to myself. It wouldn't work anyway.

Burying my face in my hands, I scrubbed the skin until it was raw. Then I put my big girl panties on and got dressed. Elic needed me to help him, and I needed to be busy. In being there for my new friend, I could take my mind off of heavier things. Things that threatened the peace I had almost found.

I dressed in soft, tan, moleskin pants, a black shirt that would hide the dirt, and comfortable flat shoes. I pulled my hair into a long tail at the base of my head before applying paints to cover the damage my tears left behind. In the kitchen, the brothers waited, dressed, and ready to go.

"We'll all walk with you, Ravena. It's a beautiful day out, and we want a chance to enjoy it for a moment," Finn said, his soft face scanning mine.

Lochlann's arms crossed over his chest, and he looked unhappy for reasons I did not understand.

"Okay," I said, feeling small and somehow more broken than I ever had in this house.

Over the hours that I been awake, I had not noticed the sky. Crazy magic sparked on the horizon, and I was transfixed by it. Purple skies and pink clouds filtered pale sunlight through them. Thunder rolled in the distance, and I wondered what bad thing rode it to us. We all stopped and stared. The whole town did.

The thunder in the distance did not detract from the swelling, terrifyingly beautiful sky. It was as if it was coming down to consume us all; it breathed and moved like a live thing. Motes danced, and lights streaked. I wondered if the world was ending. Finn sucked in a breath, and Lochlann drew a sword. Rory tensed, waiting for something to punch.

And I?

I dropped to my knees.

I knew.

Great Goddess, I knew. Whatever Seal said and whatever Ari did, I knew the truth. He was right. This knowledge would get me killed. I could never speak of it. Never. Rumors would spread, and people would talk, but I knew Ari, and I knew the truth, yet it was a truth I could never speak. Not in this land.

The magic passed, and like that, the moment was gone. The skies grew dark, and raindrops fell, first softly and then harder.

In the end, rain pounded on the streets. Water ran off of roofs and down streets in rivers.

I couldn't remember the last time it rained. Not like this. This was Goddess magic. This was the Goddess's pain and anguish raining down on us. It mixed with my anguish, and I understood why I would not see my friend for many, many seasons. It all made sense now. I wouldn't speak the words and feared even thinking them, for if the Queen knew, the world would burn.

Smiling finally, I ran, laughing and spinning under the stormy sky. I danced and sang while my mates watched, unsure and possibly thinking I'd gone mad, but my friend was free, and freedom is all any of us ever wanted. Freedom to choose. Freedom to love. Freedom to raise children without the shadow of the sword over our heads.

She was free now, and someday we would be too. It was written in the angry sky, pelting the capital in sadness, but beyond that anger was hope. I knew it. A child would save us all.

My men caught me, swinging me and dancing with me even though they did not understand my joy, and I prayed they never did. We held hands, jumped in mud puddles, and acted like fools all the way to the greenhouse. Lightning flashed but never struck, and the weather change was a beautiful, crazy thing on its own. I gloried in it even as it soaked my drawers.

The greenhouse was dark, and rain made a lovely noise beating on the glass roof. A peace so filling settled over me as I inhaled the scent of greenery and moist soil.

This place smelled so much like Rory, and I wondered if that was one of the reasons why Elic loved him. It was eerie and silent as I slipped through the aisles of plants, trees, and blooms.

I knew Elic had a small washroom in the back and hoped he had towels enough for us all. The air was heating, and the humidity would make it uncomfortable if we didn't dry off.

The brothers followed, and we headed back to the tables upon which the Queen's centerpieces rested. They were amazing. Elic might not have plant magic, but he was a true artist. The tiers of flowers were breathtaking, and the tuarceatha flowers at the top made them unforgettable. The Queen would love them.

Elic was not with his centerpieces as I would have guessed, and I assumed he was in the area behind them that had once been his home. He had rearranged the space into a floral sculpting area and a new space for seedlings. I heard a low moan and rushed forward, thinking him hurt.

Finn tried to stop me. He did. He reached for my arm, but I was too fast. I thought nothing other than that my friend was somehow injured, and so I pushed open the curtain with the brothers hot on my heels.

Elic lay on his back on top of a giant sculpting table. His legs were over the shoulders of the Queen's fair-haired guard who speared him from above. Their lips were locked in a passionate kiss, and the guard's hands wrapped around the smaller man's throat in abject possession.

The guard's other hand gripped Elic's hardness, and as he thrust into Elic, his hand pumped his cock. Elic turned to us with blissed-out eyes that changed from sated to horrified as he took us in. The guard pushed into him harder, making him cry out. As Elic came on his stomach, I turned on my heel to run out, dragging a stunned Rory with me.

Judging by his pained breathing, he missed nothing as he stood frozen in his spot. The Guard smirked at us and continued thrusting into Elic while he made eye contact with Rory. He threw his head back with a groan as he came, and Elic stilled under him, going limp. I walked through the greenhouse and out as quickly as I could without running, pulling Rory behind me. Goddess damn Elic.

I tugged Rory home. I wrapped myself around the big man as best I could and forced his leaden feet to move when he only wanted to stop. I heard his muffled cries over the pounding rain, and they broke my heart. I would strangle Elic myself for hurting him.

Why? Why now? And that it was the Queen's guard spoke of larger betrayals than just sex with another man. My hands trembled as I opened the door to our home and shoved Rory through. His brothers were not behind us as I had thought, and I imagined that they were strangling Elic for the both of us. I couldn't bring myself to care.

Inside, I stripped Rory of his soaking clothes and me of mine. I left them in a heap by the door and pushed him into my room and onto the bed, surrounding him with the only comfort I had, my skin. I covered us both and rocked him as he cried, kissing his hair and murmuring words that made no sense; they just were.

Rory, the fighter. Rory, the archer. Rory, the damaged man, finally stilled and slept after he cried his last tears.

Fucking Elic. He would pay for this.

I heard the front door open, close, and be barred. I heard the bars drop on all our doors and gave a bitter smile into Rory's sweet head. Let Elic stay out. We signed no contract.

I looked at where Rory slept against my breast and watched as his brothers came in and drop their wet clothes in a pile by my door. They joined us, wrapping up in my warm blankets and enfolding Rory with their love. Lochlann's knuckles were abraded and bleeding while gentle Finn's eyes held a dark promise. We said nothing as we held Rory, trying to soothe the sharp wounds betrayal leaves behind.

Knocks sounded at the doors that turned to furious and pounding. We did not care. We stayed in my bed until the afternoon sun filtered through my window. Only then did Rory stir. His lips found my nipple, and he suckled me like a baby might, only that soft suckle changed when he went to the other breast, teasing and nipping at the firm flesh there. Heat stirred in my core. Although it was maybe not the right thing for Rory at this moment, I let him make that choice.

The brothers stirred around us, pulling back and watching as Rory jerked me down the bed to land roughly underneath him. Parting my legs with firm hands, he prodded my flesh with his fingers; I gave way and let him in. He could take what he needed. He deserved that much. He kissed me hard, fisting my hair with his hands; he pushed into me with one stroke.

"Rory," Finn cautioned, his worried eyes on mine.

I shook my head once and reached a hand to him. He came to me, smoothing the hair from my eyes, and watched his brother as he moved inside me. Lochlann looked ready to pull Rory off, and I smiled, holding out my other hand to him as well. It might look similar to a familiar wrong often done in this house, but Rory did not rape me. He just needed so deeply at that moment that it overwhelmed him.

I gripped his hips and rose to meet his thrusts. Finally, his eyes opened, and he met mine. Wrapping my legs around his calves, I refused to let him pull away from me when he tried. He watched my face for any sign of reluctance before pushing back into me more gently.

"You don't have to be gentle, Rory. You won't hurt me," I said, bringing my hands to his face.

"I've already hurt you." He tried to pull away from me again, but I would not let go. There would be no rejection here. Not by me.

"No, Rory, you haven't," I said, meeting his eyes with mine.

Finn came between us and kissed my lips, pulling my face to his and forcing the kiss. Lochlann's head appeared in the space between Rory and me, his lips finding my breast, and Rory's eyes changed from unsure to sure. I saw the emotions play across his face like they were blown by the wind. He thrust again, and I arched into him. A hand reached between us and skimmed over my core, tightening the muscles around Rory.

Finn pushed Rory over, and I rolled with him, landing on top with a wild grin and delighted squeal. My hair fell around us like a curtain, and I rose on his hard length and pushed back down, his moans urging me on. I felt fingers run down my spine and into the hole below, causing me to cry out. A second finger joined the first, and the burning turned to pleasure when Finn's oiled length replaced his fingers and stretched me to new limits. Gripping my shoulders and pinning them in place, he slid delicately into that spot no one had ever been. I rocked my hips against Rory's, unable to be still.

Hands tugged at my hair, and Lochlann pushed my mouth to his cock. I sucked it hard, wanting everything he had to give and more. I wanted them all, and I was never sharing them again. Never. Everything they had to give was mine, and I wanted it.

I rode Rory hard, giving him what he needed but would not take for himself. His brothers sharing the experience would take any doubt Rory felt and push it away. I appreciated them, and I'm sure that their motives were completely altruistic.

I came, clenching Rory and Finn so tight that they sucked in a shared breath and stilled my hips. When it passed and my muscles eased, I chased it again. Grinding and writhing against them both until Rory lost the battle, pushing his seed deep inside of me. Finn followed behind him, and still, I rode them both as their fluids leaked from around their softening flesh. When Lochlann's tip breached my throat and his balls hit my chin, I came apart. Crying out and bucking like a mad thing, I drank him down, my hands clutching at his back as his shouts echoed off the walls of the room.

I sagged onto Rory. His arms wrapped around me in a tender embrace. Fluids, sweat, and other things soaked our skin and the sheets around us, but no one cared. We lay like that for hours, letting the heartbreak change into something else.

When the sun dipped below the horizon, Lochlann rose. A damp chill had settled into the place, and he lit hearth fires for us. Slowly we stirred. One by one, we kissed, rose, bathed, and returned to bed. We said nothing, not yet. We weren't ready.

Rain still fell. The violent deluge shifted to something softer, and the sound of it on our metal roof lulled me. Dinner appeared from Miri, and we stuffed ourselves before going back to bed. Intermittent banging on our doors jarred our peace, but we ignored it. There would be time later to deal with it but now was not the time. When finally we were ready to go back to sleep, we piled into my bed, wrapped our arms one around another, and slept in a naked pile of arms and legs.

During the night, each one of them awoke and made love to me, the others grunting and shuffling out of the way in their sleep. I knew Rory by his smell and calloused hands, Finn by the soft fall of his bangs onto mine, and Lochlann by the hard planes of his muscles and the depth of love he poured into me as he gave me all of himself.

We were one- finally. This is what it meant to be mated. It didn't mean that we would always agree. It didn't even mean that we would always get along. It just meant that when bad things happened, we would be there for one another. That is the meaning of the bond we share.

I was alone when I rose, sticky and slick from their combined fluids. Stumbling into the washroom, I soaked for a long while in the hottest water I could. The muffled voices of the brothers talking low came from the kitchen, and the sound of bodies moving about the house could be heard from down the hall.

When I went to my room to dress, I found that it had been straightened and crusty sheets replaced with clean. My floor had been swept, and the dresser wiped down. It smelled fresh and clean again. I would go to Miri's today for the lunch crowd. The distraction would be great, and I needed to work off all the meals she had been feeding us.

The kitchen was quiet when I walked in. Clean plates sat in the sink, and only Finn remained.

"They went to work," he said, coming to meet me. "Are you okay?" he asked.

"Of course, I'm okay, Finn. What of Rory?" I asked, my stomach clenching on itself as nausea rippled through.

"Rory will be fine. We intend to ask the Queen to rescind Elic's invitation to share our home, and as we have signed no contract, we think she will concede.

Nodding once, I added, "I will speak to him at some point. He needs to understand that he is not welcome here. Not anymore."

"I don't think that is a wise idea. He can't be trusted." Finn said, watching my face.

"No, he can't, but I will speak to him anyway, and if you box his things up, I will take them to him." I brushed his long bangs from his eyes so that I could see them both. Where they usually were clear and blue, today they were cloudy like the skies outside.

247

"Ravena," he started.

"No, Finn. I will speak to him. He doesn't get to do this to us. To all of us." I laid my head on his chest, listening to his heartbeat.

"No. I agree; he doesn't," Finn said with a long sigh. "Are you working today?" he asked.

"Yes, if everyone else is working, then so am I." I pulled from him and ate the breakfast he laid out for me.

"I'm moving the last of my things here from my shop. After today, I'll work from home." He took my plate when I was done and washed it, placing it with the others.

"That's wonderful. You should take Elic's room and turn it into your workroom instead of building something outside," I said, hiding the hint of pain I felt behind a bright smile. I couldn't believe I'd been fooled by him.

"That's not a bad idea, love. We shall see," he said as he walked down the hallway to gather Elic's things.

I was almost done cleaning up the kitchen when Finn called me to him. Even from this distance, I heard him suck in his breath and went to him quickly.

"What is it?" I asked, storming into Elic's former space.

He sat on the edge of the bed with a box in his hands. The look on his face was dark, and his eyes furious. I went to him, trying to take the box, but he wrestled against me to keep it from my hands.

"Finn, what is it?" I said again, wresting the box from him. I set it beside us, and my eyes widened when I glanced inside.

"It was under his bed," he said, bringing his hard eyes to mine. Finn, usually the soft one, scared me with that look.

I pulled my hummingbird hairpin from the box. Followed by the shift Rory had given me that was streaked in dried come. It smelled of Rory and me. And something else. Elic. It smelled of him too. A shiver ran down my spine. A stiff rag came next, and I knew what had made it stiff. My hairbrush was in the box, as well as some of my underthings, breast bands, and ribbons. He had some of my clothes and a few strands of my hair in a glass container. I stilled.

"What?" I couldn't finish the question. Tears formed in my eyes, and I felt more violated than I ever had by Rowan.

"I don't know. Elic is obsessed with you." He scrubbed his hands over his face, and when he looked back at me, he seemed years older.

"He doesn't want me. Not like that," I rushed to say.

"Maybe he wants to be you. I don't understand it either, but he is dangerous. I know you want to talk to him, but you aren't going alone. I swore never to clip your beautiful wings, but I can't allow that. I'm sorry." Taking the box from me, he sat me on his lap and soothed my hair. We would get through this. We all would.

After a long moment, he placed me on the side of the bed. Rising, he took the butterfly pin and my hairbrush from the box before throwing the rest of it in the fireplace to burn. Tugging me behind him, he closed the door to the room, carrying only what Elic had brought with him and nothing more.

## Chapter Thirty-Seven

### Finn

The look on Ravena's face gutted me. She could not hide her emotions, and they rippled across her like the surface of a lake on a stormy day. She wanted so badly to confront Elic, and I wanted no part of his life to touch her again. What a fucked up situation.

"It's my fault," she said. "It was my idea for him to come."

"No. None of this is your fault," I said as we stepped out into the warm spring sun and pulled our door closed behind us. I took the metal key we never used and locked it behind me, stiff tumblers locking in place. "We all had the same idea and thought it would work. We couldn't be sure any man could be trusted but believed that Elic was a good choice. Now we know."

"What? She just assigns another. And another. I can't do this again. I can't. I don't want anyone else. I want only you three." Her breath hitched in her chest, and misery seeped out of her very pores. "I am nothing. I have no choice, no design, and no recourse. My life is of no consequence."

I pulled her around so sharply that her head snapped back. "You will never repeat those words, Ravena. Never. You are everything. At least to us. We will never accept another into our home, and you will be safe. We will all be safe. That is the end of it." I did not intend for my voice to be razor-sharp, but it was. Her eyes widened even as her skin paled.

"But."

"No. We don't talk about it, and I understand why, Ravena, but we love you. We all love you. We are in love with you and are absolutely crazy over you. You are the world to us as no other could ever be; we were made for you and you alone. Never again will we put you at risk with a stranger. We are yours, and we will see to your safety.

The Queen will understand or not, but there will never be another of the Queen's spies in our home." I crushed her to me and kissed her hard. Her chest heaved against me, and I didn't care if every soul in Talamh na Sithe heard the words, for I meant them.

She was everything. She was the world. To us, there was nothing else that mattered.

She ended the kiss, pulling away and nodding once. Her blue eyes turned fierce as we came closer to the greenhouse. She would say her piece, and we would leave Elic behind as part of our troubled history to become a distant memory.

Even Rory had begun to doubt himself and his feelings for Elic; I had seen it on his face when he looked at the other man. We would move on from this, and our lives would be better. Ravena pushed aside the door of the greenhouse and called Elic's name. I leaned against the wall, my hands near the short sword I had strapped under my loose tunic.

He came rushing from the back, stopping short when he saw me. His yellow eyes narrowed on me, then rounded on Ravena.

"Let me explain," he begged her, coming forward.

I moved from the wall, straightening, and he stopped his approach.

"Please, listen. The man I told you about, the one I was asking about poison for. It was me. Cuin Bas has been after me for months. I'm not safe with him. I need help." How he lied, I don't know, but he did, at least in some part.

"Stop," she screamed at him, slapping his cheek so that it jerked to the side. "You lie. I saw your face. You gave yourself to him completely. Your eyes were black with pleasure. Don't tell me. Don't tell *me* that it was rape. Do not, Elic. There is no fucking poison. For once and for all, go tell the Queen. Go tell her guards. I care not what you do from this moment forward; you are dead to me and dead to my mates. It's over. Stay away from us." She dropped the box containing his things on the ground and tugged me, stunned, behind her.

Our little bird has talons. Sharp ones. As kind and gentle as she is, her spine is made of steel.

No.

It is made of unbreakable glass.

I had never been more proud of another person in all my days. All this time, I thought she would forgive anything.

I was wrong.

Her hair flew around her in inky clouds, and thunder replaced misery on her face. She smelled of ozone and fury. She was angry, and I never wanted to be on the other end of the depth of it. At Miri's, I left her, going home to finish cleaning out Elic's room and remove the stain of distrust and betrayal that we had invited into our lives.

I heard the front door open, close, and small feet scurry down the hall and heard her rustling around a bit in her room. I stepped into the hallway to see if she was okay. She had changed clothes and now wore the soft blue dress that matched her eyes and made her skin look Goddess touched.

"I spilled sauce on my clothes and didn't want to wear them through lunch when it is still so early." She came forward, her blue eyes troubled. She kissed my lips before rushing back the way she came.

Going to the door, I watched as she hustled the few yards back to Miri's, her blue dress billowed, caught in the stiff wind brought on by yet another storm, and moved around her like smoke. Heading back to my new workshop, I paused at her door. Looking around to make sure I was alone, I went into her room, shutting it behind me.

# Chapter Thirty-Eight

## Lochlann

I would go to the Queen even though Rory was now the oldest of the family and our head. I would ask to rescind our petition to have Elic join our home. I would not go today. Today, I was so angry and my thoughts so dark that I dared speak to no one.

During training, I picked the biggest, meanest son of a bitch to spar with and pounded my fists into him, relishing when he found my flesh. The pain cleared my head, and I could think again. Our schedule was full, and I would not make the diner for lunch. I worried less with Finn close to home, but with Elic and the Queen's guards skulking around, I worried anyway.

After training, my assignment was to clear a fallen tree from the main road on the capital's east side. I went with my unit; an ax slung over my shoulder. The stiff, cool breeze felt good on my skin and spoke of another storm coming. I felt it appropriate. When the unit passed my house, I ducked in. Sparring had left blood on my shirt, and I wanted to change it, hoping still to be able to catch Ravena at the end of her lunch shift. And if we cleared the tree fast enough, it might be possible.

I went past Ravena's door on my way to the washroom then stopped. Backing slowly, I listened. At the back of the house where Elic once stayed, I heard furniture being moved, likely Finn making the room his own. I needed to hurry and catch my unit before they cared that I was missing, but I paused anyway. Slipping sideways into Ravena's room, I shut the door behind me.

## Chapter Thirty-Nine

### Rory

Heat seared my thoughts, and all I could see was black rage. Not because I loved Elic. Not because he had fucked another man. I raged because Ravena cared for him, and he betrayed her on a deeper level than she recognized. Elic and the Queen's guard. That was not a coincidence. The questions about suspected abuse and Rowan's death. His obsession with Ari and her potions. It all made sense.

At the very least, he spied for his lover, but if I allowed myself to believe that, then I had also to think that the Queen had sent him from the beginning to trap us. We had known it could happen. I just hadn't known it would come from the man I once loved. The man I had, once upon a time, wanted to spend the rest of my life with. Wanted to make my mate and share eternity with.

No more.

Arrows flew with deadly precision upon the target downfield. Magic thrummed through me, raising the hair on my arms. Ozone took the place of oxygen, and I felt the storm coming. I wanted to go to Ravena. I needed her. Last night, my behavior scared me, and I forced myself to stay away until the edge of darkness in my soul eased, and I could trust myself again.

I would never hurt her. Not intentionally, but I could hurt her trying to soothe the razor's edge of pain, searing my soul, and I could not allow that. I loved her. Goddess, I loved her. She made me into something I am not. She made me stronger. She took the edges of my wounds and molded them like clay into the semblance of a whole person that has not been ripped apart by violence. She gave me something I never knew I needed and now would die before I lost- something that I would kill for.

I loosed another arrow and split the one I had shot before in half. Over and over, my arrows rained down on the target, and I let them fly. Men avoided me, and no one approached as the cloud of darkness suffocating me kept them at bay. Tension eased through the string I pulled, and slowly, arrow after arrow, my mind cleared, and my tightened muscles eased.

I put my bow down and angled toward the boxing rings where men sparred. Silence met me as all eyes turned. I was no stranger to these rings, but there were few left that would lift their fists against me. Then I saw Lann.

Lann is a mountain of dark-skinned Fae. Muscles rippled over his bare, tattooed flash, and despair leaked from him on his breath. He was one of Airmed's mates and had not been seen since her disappearance. I did not know him well, but I knew the scent of unchained fury that rolled off of him. I knew that Ravena loved Airmed, and I loved Ravena. This man, I knew. I recognized something within him. I stepped into the ring and met his eyes, seeing my own reflected off their black depths.

He grinned in understanding before he brought his mass to bear on me. And we fought. We fought with kicks, punches, and jabs. We fought until blood ran down both our faces and smeared on our chests, neither backing down. Surrounded by more and more of the Queen's troops, we fought until our muscles were lax, and the darkness was gone from both our souls.

Clasping forearms and breaking apart, I knew I had found a friend to last a lifetime. Possibly the only friend I've ever had outside of my family group. After bathing off the blood in the Laconia by the old barracks, we talked. We talked for hours, our voices hushed and covered by the hot water that poured into and out of the bathhouse, taking our bloodied castoff away.

We talked of war and treason. The words we said could bring both our families a painful death if anyone heard them. We blamed the Queen.

Aramea had ruined this place, taking our magic and killing our children. She was the rot that permeated this land. We talked of armies and coups. The Queen would die, and when she did, our mates would be free to have children. Boys and girls would once again run in the streets, and the Goddess would give us more of them than we could handle. Someday. Someday when this Queen was gone, and another ruler has taken her place.

Lann said Airmed would be Queen. Ravena had whispered the same more than once. Maybe it was true. For now, though, we would fuel the trickle of sedition until it became a mighty river and cleansed this place of all that was wrong with it.

Lann walked me home. We stood outside Airmed's darkened bakery, and I watched as he pressed his palm to the glass. Closing his eyes, he leaned his forehead against it and shuddered a breath out. I blamed the Queen for this too. We could not be what we were meant to be under her rule. None of us.

"What will you do, Lann?" I asked, watching him grieve his mate.

"Survive. We will all survive until the day comes when we can live. That is what I'll do." He whistled, and his horse came to him, ghosted by the mare that spoke of Airmed. He waved goodbye and kicked his stallion away from town.

The house was empty that I could see. A silver key lay on the table, and I took it, knowing that never again would we keep our doors open to the land. Never again. I pulled my bloodied shirt over my head and tossed it into the hearth fire that glowed in the living room. It was beyond repair.

Like me.

I bypassed my room and went to Ravena's. Her bed was neatly made, and her room spotless. The small rug she covered her floor with was pushed up in the middle, and I bent to tug it flat. The hump in the rug caught on something, and I pulled harder, hearing it snag.

Lifting the rug, I found a board; one edge just barely lifted above the others. Rising slowly with a look into the hall, I shut myself in her room and then removed the board in her floor.

# Chapter Forty

## Ravena

Rory was the last to filter in. By unspoken agreement, we met at Miri's. I worked through lunch and, not ready to go home, stayed for the dinner crowd. The restaurant was packed, and my help was appreciated. My men sat huddled at a corner table, remnants of multiple meals in front of them.

After having it out with Elic, I felt better, even if I could see they did not. We would get through this and move on. Again.

Rory walked through the diner, his eyes sparking and muscles languid. With feline grace, he parted the crowd, fresh cuts on his, and Lochlann's face told me how they had blown off their excess steam. Finn still vibrated with fury, and I would take it from him in the way females have since the beginning of time. We all have weapons; some just wield them differently.

Then we could heal.

Miri stopped and spoke with them often. I shook my head at her attempts to lighten their moods. They chuckled with her, and rare phrases would reach my ears.

Often they said they told her so, and I wondered what they meant, knowing that it had to be how much of a help I would be to her. I blushed with their praise, for they are right. I am needed here.

Tonight's special was a rare fish from the depths of a lake in Troll country. Not only is it dangerous to obtain, but it is also dangerous to prepare and eat. Miri showed me a dozen times how to cut the venom glands out of the fish before dipping it in egg, flour, spices, and frying it. She watched closely as I prepped fish after fish. Only once did I accidentally puncture the gland and release the dark green venom within. She threw that fish in the alley, and immediately, three very large Fae rats died after falling upon it in hunger.

This fish was serious business.

I wondered if it was an ingredient Ari used.

My hands shook as I took the brothers' plates of death fish surrounded by salted, buttered cabbage and potatoes. I brought cups of ale and glasses of tea. They ate ravenously, laughing and talking well into the evening. As the lunch crowd thinned, I folded my apron and joined them. I picked bites of fish off their plates and drank two glasses of ale to ease the muscles in my back and legs.

Rory dropped the fork he held with the last bite of fish on it and glared at the door. Our table silenced at his arrival even as the rest of the diner did not.

Unsure, Elic stood in the doorway watching us. Rory started to rise, and I beat him to it.

"What do you want, Elic," I whispered when I got to him, shooting a direct order with my eyes to stay where they were to my mates.

"You aren't usually here for dinner, Ravena. I come here all the time. There's no way I could have known," he said, his voice low and sharp.

"Fine. We'll leave," I said, turning from him.

"And let the Queen's guards know there's trouble in paradise?" he asked. He turned his yellow eyes to mine and showed me his real face, and it was not a good one.

In the corner, I saw the Queen's notorious henchmen watching us with avid attention. I felt the blood drain from my face.

"Now," he started. "You will serve your mate dinner, and then we will all go home. So says the Queen." His eyes narrowed, and a flood of hate so strong emanated from him that it shook me.

My breath caught in my throat, and he pushed past, joining the brothers at their table. I froze. Miri's eyes met mine, and I knew not what to do. Miri threw my apron at me with a wink, and I caught it.

Slowly I came back to myself. I brought the brothers fresh tea and dropped a glass off for Elic. Their table was silent as the men seethed. There was no conversation. Elic ordered the fish, and I brought it, wishing I had not thrown the improperly cut one away. One bite. One. That was all it would take.

He tried to speak to the others, and they would not engage. They would also not make a scene with Elic's lover and the Queen's chief torturer just a few paces away. It was uncomfortable, to say the least. I filled glasses and served as I'd been told.

Finn slipped away out the back door, and I knew he meant to guard our home. Miri nodded as I went for more tea, and I took the hint and left as well. No good could come from this. I heard Elic yell for me just as I slipped through the door to the house, Rory and Lochlann pounded after, and Finn barred the door behind them.

Elic hit the door hard, screaming. His words were unintelligible, but the ones we could understand spoke of rage, jealousy, and hate. He hated me.

He may have loved Rory once upon a time, but he hated me more. In his mind, I had taken Rory from him. The men wanted to confront him, but that would lead to nothing good. If they left this house, they would rip him apart piece by piece. Elic's fists pounded at the door, and his mouth spewed hate. He threw stones, then bricks at the window glass, but Finn had made it, and it would not be broken.

Then a voice, low and commanding, told him to leave. Breathing a sigh of relief, we watched as he was led from our door by his lover. A confrontation would come, and this would be dealt with, but now was not the time. The anger was too fresh and would lead to a disastrous and possibly murderous outcome if not left to ebb. We did not speak as we moved through the house, preparing for bed with solemn thoughts and darkened minds.

I lay on my bed alone, my body sore from standing on my feet for more hours than I was used to. The front door opened and closed. The garden door opened and closed. The house had a restless feel to it that I understood all too well. Anticipation weighed heavily on the place, and I wondered: I lay there and wondered.

Thunder sounded in the distance, and I did something I have not done in many weeks; I pulled my door shut. Restless and needing to be away from the weight of the pain around me, I slipped through my window and out into the night.

# Chapter Forty-One

## Finn

Like a wraith, I slipped through the front door and into the darkened living room. The hearth fire burned low, and I did not stoke it. The storm outside had brought warm, muggy air, making the small space oppressive. I did not open any windows.

Scooting down the hall on the tips of my toes, I paused. We had allowed Elic to make a mockery of us at dinner, but what of it? To anyone not in the know, Ravena approached him, and he joined us at our table. No, we were not effusive with our affections or boisterous in our talk after his arrival. Still, to outward appearances, nothing would have been amiss.

And that is good.

Every door along the hall was closed, and the house had an empty feel to it. Concerned, I changed into dry sleep pants and toweled my hair off. After I went to each door and, one by one opened them.

No one was here, not even Ravena.

The house was empty.

Ice knifed through my heart, and I felt like I might drop at that moment. I could walk the town, but I knew I'd find nothing. Not yet. Instead, I forced myself to my room, picked up a book, and waited.

Sometime during the wee hours of the morning, exhaustion took me. I awoke, sweating and screaming into the darkness, only to feel Ravena's cold, rain-soaked body slide in behind mine. Immediately the nightmare eased and was gone.

She slipped her birdlike hands under my ribs and pulled me to her. Thunder continued to sound in the distance, and rain fell on the roof. Her warm breath ruffled the hairs on the back of my neck, and she rocked me back to sleep until a loud banging on the door woke me the next morning.

I rose on my elbow to find that my bed was full. At some point during the night, Ravena, Lochlann, and Rory had piled in with me, and there was not an empty spot left on my small mattress. I pushed myself up to my elbow, trying to find the limbs that belonged to me and pull them free.

"By order of the Queen, open this door!" Sounded from the front of the house, and I froze. Around me, the others stirred.

"The Queen is here," I whispered, urging them awake.

I rose from the bed and drew on my pants before peeking out of the glass to see that the Queen was, indeed, on our doorstep. I unbarred the door, opening it as the others padded into the living with bleary faces and tired eyes. Lochlann shouldered ahead of Ravena, effectively blocking her.

"Where is your fourth mate?" the Queen asked. "Where is Elic."

We looked around, confused for a moment, still shaking sleep from our heads.

"Not here, I suppose," I said, watching the others from the corner of my eye.

"Perhaps he's at work?" Ravena mumbled, no doubt irritated about being awakened so soon after she went to sleep. As were my brothers. As was I. "He has been working on your centerpieces," she finished with a yawn.

"Elic is dead," the Queen said, watching our faces.

No one said a word. Eventually, Ravena shook her head as if confused, adding, "What did you say?"

"I said," The Queen enunciated every word. "Elic is dead."

"How?" I asked.

"None of you seem surprised that I have just told you your fourth mate is dead." Her head tilted in a slow, reptilian manner.

"Your Highness, we are barely awake, and we are trying to make sense of your words. What happened?"

"Why don't you tell me?" she asked, watching us through narrowed eyes. Regardless of what happened, we must be cautious, and I knew it.

"The last we saw, he was walking away from Miri's with Cuin Bas. They are lovers," Rory said, his voice sharp and laced with the pain he felt.

The Queen sucked in a sharp breath and skewered the pale guard with her eyes.

"Last night, we ate dinner together at Miri's while Ravena finished her shift, Elic ate with us, and we waited for him to finish. We found out about Elic and your guard just the day before, and we were trying to work through that since living together is still so new. Elic left with him after," I said, shrugging my shoulders as if to say I hadn't seen him since.

Her eyes glittered as they turned to the man next to her. He said nothing but trained his glare on us.

"It was them, your Grace; they did to him what they did to Rowan," he offered with a sneer at Ravena.

"We did nothing to Rowan," Lochlann said, not lying. We did nothing to Rowan- Ravena did.

The Queen kept her gaze trained on her guard, "And how do you know he was found bent over his work tables, Cuin? Is that your seed on his back then?"

"I," he stopped, shutting his mouth.

"We will speak of this later," she said, and from the look on her face, I knew there would be more than speaking going on. The Queen's punishments were notorious.

"Who cooked the fish served at Miri's last night, Ravena?" she asked, her cold stare turning to the pale bird next to me.

"Miri and I both did," she answered softly.

"Who prepared it?" the Queen asked, her back stiff and arms tense.

"Miri and I both did, your Highness," Ravena answered, fighting to keep the tremble from her voice.

"Who plated and served Elic his meal?" The Queen tilted her head again and went still in the manner of a snake waiting to strike.

"Miri plated the meal, and I served it," Ravena whispered.

"Those are the same answers Miri gave us during her interrogation. All you say aligns with her words. Elic was poisoned, I have no doubt, but I cannot say if it was one of my dearly departed daughter's poisons that killed him or a fish from Miri's diner. I will find out. I will, and when I do, you will suffer if it is by your hand that Elic died. His family is loyal to the crown, and they want blood," she paused. "Search the house and take Ravena. She's yours now." She turned, and the tall, dark-haired guard grabbed Ravena, jerking her to him.

His hands ran down the thin shift she wore, and he stopped, pinching her nipple. She let out a scream and began to fight him.

"I'll have fun breaking this one," the dark-haired guard spoke for the first time that I had ever heard.

Ravena began fighting harder, and the guard slapped her face, sending her to the floor. The light-haired guard pulled his sword as we stepped forward as one to pull her to us.

"We have a contract, my Queen," Lochlann said, going to Ravena's side despite the blade at his throat.

"I care not for the contract. Not when you make me look like a fool in front of the people I rule. The contract was signed with Rowan as head of this house. He is gone now. I consider the contract null and void," she spat on Ravena, turning from us as the guard grabbed her and jerked her to him again.

His hands ripped her shift from her body, exposing her to him, and he pushed her against the back of the sofa. I watched his cock hardening in his pants as he pushed himself between her thighs, and I moved to my sword. So did my brothers. We might die, but no man would touch our mate whom she did not invite to touch her. No man. That choice was hers.

"Stop," Ravena yelled. "Stop. If you hurt me, I could lose my baby." The room stilled, and everyone froze.

"You cannot lie. You are bred?" The Queen turned from our door, her eyes boring through our mate. My brothers and I turned too, for this was information we did not know.

Ravena stood naked, her body bared by the guard for all to see. His fingers stilled just outside her entrance. Were her breasts a bit heavier? Yes, they seemed to be, and her pink nipples a bit darker. Was there a roundness to her womb that I had not noticed? Yes. Yes, there was, just a hint of a swell to her. Her face was too pale, and her eyes glazed with unshed tears.

"I won't break her then; just let me use her. Let me test the veracity of her words," the dark guard pushed his fingers into Ravena, and the room erupted when she screamed.

Rory stepped up to his mate and threw the man off of Ravena as he pulled her to him. Her body disappearing in his arms so that he covered her completely. He turned with her, taking her to his room and barring the door.

"She is ours, and you will not take her from us. You will not," I said, putting my body between the Queen, her men, and the entrance to the hallway down which Rory fled.

"When she is heavy with child, she will be mine anyway. As will the child. You know this. It's in the contract you speak so often about.

"No." Finn's face fell, and his body stiffened.

"Perhaps you should read the document you signed," the Queen said; she smirked, making her face ugly.

"She is ours," Lochlann said. "The baby is ours."

"If it is male, you will be allowed to raise it for a short time. You know this. If it is female, it is mine. I will raise it, as I raised The Eight. Your daughter will be another Ravena as she is the future of Talamh na Sithe."

My heart stilled, and the true depravity of the Queen was shown to me. We were never going to be allowed to be a family. Our child would be killed or forced to follow in her mother's footsteps. Given away. Beaten. Raped. Taught to cry for a man's pleasure and with no recourse other than three angry fathers that would be superfluous to the Queen. Expendable. Murdered.

Rory's words earlier were sharp in my mind. The ones he whispered at the diner hidden under the din of other easy conversations. The words about revolution and war. This Queen must die. I thought him crazy at the time, but he was right. She cannot be allowed to live and rule any longer.

He said there was a plan and that with time- with time, there would be change. Give it thirty years. Time for our child to be old enough to face his or her fate at the hands of this Queen. Thirty years is time to raise a child to near maturity. Why thirty years and not now.

Why?

And then it hit me. Airmed was pregnant too. Oh my Goddess, Ari had run. The storms, the strange skies, the magic over the land that had vanished as quickly as it came. Ari and Ravena were pregnant. That's where the hope lay — our children.

Ari had taken that strange magic and run. She had taken her unborn child to freedom. I knew it. No doubt Ravena knew it.

The Queen, if she did not know now, would figure it out. It wasn't all that hard. People would die.

Build an army, Rory had said. Build an army in secret and wait... wait for a new Queen. Someone strong enough to take down Aramea, for that's who she is. Just Aramea. She was no longer my Queen. Who was? Airmed or her child? I did not care.

Ravena said Airmed was the strongest of us all and would someday be Queen, but the strong feel of strange magic made me think it would be her child. I did not care as long as it brought change. Change for the better. Change for all of us. Freedom for our children. Maybe even for us if we survived the insurrection.

I lowered my eyes so that the truth would not show through in them.

"Leave us," I said. "Leave us to tend to our mate and our child.

"Babies are fragile in this land," Lochlann echoed my deepest fear. Life was so fragile here. "Do not upset her further and pray to the Goddess your Ogre's rough handling and touching what is not his to touch does not make her lose this baby, or you have my word he will die," Lochlann glared, his hands on his short sword.

"I will forgive your impertinence and your threat, only because fatherhood makes males protective. She is yours. For now, she is yours. Guard her well or face my punishment." She turned, took her men, and left.

I sagged against the wall in relief, even as a sob left my throat. Lochlann came to me and wrapped his arms around me.

"Well done, brother. Well done," he said, comforting me as I struggled to stand. Confrontation is difficult for me. I really am a lover, not a fighter. But when it mattered most, finally, finally, I had stood up for Ravena as had we all.

"Is it true? I asked, hope leaking into my words.

"She cannot lie, not that I know of. Her statement left no room for omission or misinterpretation that I can find. Come, let us find out." He unwrapped himself from me, and together, we walked to find out the truth.

# Chapter Forty-Two

## Rory

I held Ravena as she cried. Rocking her side to side the way she does when I am screaming into the night. I murmured words I don't remember to calm her. I hummed tunelessly when words failed me. Shaking, she covered her nakedness with a sheet and let me hold her. Clutching herself between her thin legs where the guard had forced his fingers into her.

I would kill that guard, I promised myself, and I promised Ravena as she cried herself to sleep in my arms. I felt the promise settle over us as the Goddess accepted it as truth. I would kill him.

Lann was right. There would be war, and he would die at my hands for touching Ravena against her will. She had a choice, and I would die for her right to exercise it. Our baby had a choice, and I would die for that too. That's what mates do. And that is what fathers do.

Determination so strong settled over me that my spine stiffened from the imagined pain of it.

A soft knock sounded at my door, and Ravena cried out in fear, shattering my heart. I had not done enough, fast enough.

Not really. In the end, I had, but after. Only after. Tears slipped into her hair from my eyes. Never again. I rocked her harder and cried for both of us.

The knock sounded again. "Please, Rory, let us in. When you can, let us in. They understood.

When I recovered my senses, I let out a ragged breath and picked Ravena up, carrying her to the door with me to raise the bar I had never lowered in this house, not once. Only Rowan had been allowed a bar on his door, and I had listened to Ravena scream alone behind it more than once.

Never again.

I raised the bar and let my brothers in. All of us were hers. She owned us. She had been given no choice in coming here, but she owned us now. They would pry her from my cold and dead hands, and I would kill her myself before they would get to her. She would want that. I made that promise, and the Goddess accepted it as well.

We would get through this. Like we always did. We would get through it together.

My brothers rushed in, and Lochlann ripped Ravena from my arms, delicately so as not to wake her. She moaned then settled in. After Lochlann rocked her more and checked her for injuries, Finn stole her from him. We said nothing. Not one word, just held her between us, in silence.

As darkness took the day away, she stirred, pushing and begging us to take it away.

"I still feel him, please, make it stop," she cried over and over.

I bent my head between her thighs and licked the stain of him away. She sighed, more in relief than pleasure. Finn bent his head to her nipples, and Lochlann stared at her beautiful face, watching, pushing her hair aside when it tried to hide her true face from us.

I slipped inside her first. I couldn't stop myself. I needed to feel her and to know that she was okay. That she would be okay. I felt the hard knot of her cervix as I bumped against it. It was hard now. Protecting our child from intrusion, but her body accepted me, melted into mine, and found pleasure from my own. She cried out, and I drank her cry in with my kisses.

Lochlann wiped the hair from her face, and Finn lay next to her, his hands tracing down the lines of her body where mine allowed.

She wrapped her arms around me, locking her legs over mine, and pushed herself into me, taking over, riding me hard even though I was above her. When she came, she tightened around me so hard that my balls drew up instantly and emptied into her. She shattered under me and came together again, even more beautiful than she had been the moment before.

I would figure this thing out. I would find a way to withstand her soaking folds and wring orgasm after orgasm out of her. I would. Until then, I slid beside her as Finn flipped her over and on top of him. She sighed as she settled over his thick cock, rocking into him immediately to take him. It might be weird to some that I enjoyed watching my brother's cock slide in and out my mate even as my own come dripped out of her body.

To me, it was normal, beautiful even. We are a family. One unit with a shared purpose. Lochlann, being unable to wait anymore, shoved his dick into her mouth, and I chuckled when she gave me a wink.

She knew she was gorgeous and more so at that moment than any other. I watched her come again and swallow Lochlann down as Finn bucked against her once more and filled her to overflowing. When he was as done as I was going to let him be, I pulled her to me and snuggled her under the hollow of my chin. They moved around, rising and righting things, lighting fires, and barring doors, but I held her tight, refusing to move with her sleeping under my chin. Her breath tickled the thin hairs on my chest, and when my brothers returned and settled around me, I slept too.

# Chapter Forty-Three

## Ravena

We settled into an uneasy peace with the land. Aramea was so busy chasing rumors of Airmed that she seemed to forget about us, and we did our best to keep it that way.

Despite their protests, I continued to work for Miri a few hours a week but never returned to the greenhouse. Elic's family would have screamed more loudly for blood if they were forced to see me more often than they did.

The mystery of how Elic died was never solved. The guard was blamed publicly by the Queen, but there was talk.

Too much talk.

She said it was an accident and did not send another man to our home, not that any would have come unless ordered. Our household was rumored to be dangerous to outsiders, and that suited us just fine.

We'll never know which of us killed Elic. I am only confident that we all tried. Four black bottles went missing from the supposedly secret spot under my floor. Four black bottles. Not one. Not three. Four. In this thing, we were united, though we never speak of it. Then again, maybe the fish killed him. Those venom glads were easily missed.

Perhaps Elic went down in history as the most poisoned Fae ever to be poisoned, who can say. The only question I would have been interested in the answer to was who had brought Elic to his final orgasm? Not that I cared. I cared not one bit.

I desperately hoped it was Rory who fucked him to death.

We settled into our home and our routine. I was, indeed, pregnant, and despite my willowy genetics, my belly rounded and grew. It rounded until the day I awoke to a rush of blood and other things as my womb emptied itself of life. I stared as it flowed out of me, feeling numb and maybe not as horrified as I should have been.

I hadn't meant to get pregnant. I had forgotten to take my potion once. Just one time. I was not ungrateful for the gift of a child, and I was happy to know that it was possible, but after the incident with the Queen and her guards, I knew that no matter what, our child would not be safe. Boy or girl, their blood would hasten the death of this wretched land as it soaked into the soil.

I cried; I did. That little piece of my mates leaving me hurt more than I knew possible, but it was for the best in the end.

I would never forget the potion again, and as long as The Eight, now Six, wanted it, I would make it. Ari had included the recipe in the bag full of glass vials. The choice would always be ours, and I chose not to think about another child until Talamh na Sithe was free. The brothers understood.

We held each other and cried over our loss, but we understood. We agreed on this and most things. Someday, stacks of black-haired blue-eyed children would pile up on beds, fight, play, and be free. Not today, though. We had time to do it right and would be patient. We wanted our girls and boys to play with girls and boys from all over Talamh na Sithe without fear and without doubt.

A funny thing happened amid the turmoil surrounding my coming into their home. Somewhere, somehow along the way in the dark of night on the edge of the storm that seemed ever present in our lives, we fell in love. Honest love. Real love. Scarred love. Not fairy tale love.

It wasn't instant, and it wasn't easy. But love being always impatient but never unkind, crept into our lives anyway, taking root like a vine in our hearts. As vines are my magic, I tended the thing, and it grew, blooming into something extraordinary. Something so strong and thick that it could never be uprooted.

We are happy.

We found peace.

Together we are family.

And someday, we will be free.

Dear Reader,

Reviews are the lifeblood of every author, big and small. If you read a book, consider reviewing it. You might help someone find their new favorite author!

What's next? Goddess Bound, the last book in the Healer series, is hot on the heels of Ravena, but Teagan may need to get her story out before Lara finishes hers. We'll see what the voices in my head say. Lara isn't ready to say goodbye just yet, so she keeps giving me push back when I go to end her story. There's something so powerful about beginnings, but endings have a certain power too. I just need Lara to see it that way. There's also an Omegaverse book that is just about done (those characters were PUSHY, let me tell you that.) There's always something cooking and usually more than one something. Follow me on social media for updates.

~ Sharilyn

Sharilyn spent most of her early years on the Grand Strand of South Carolina, annoying local police officers and probably pretty much everyone else. She graduated from the University of South Carolina and now lives on a small farm outside of Morgantown, WV, with various farm animals, her husband, and three kids who love to annoy her. (Karma is a bitch).

Sharilyn writes Urban Fantasy, Omegaverse, and Reverse Harem, and loves showing Quarter horses, trail riding, reading, and being annoyed by her kids. If she is missing, check for her horse trailer. If it is missing, no worries, she'll be back. Probably.

**Healer Series: Series Complete**

Cerridwen's Tears

Healer

House of Fire

The Scarlet Heron

The Flame Keeper

Goddess Bound

**The Eight Series:**

Airmed

Ravena

Teagan

**The Omegas of the New South:**

The Omega Rule

The Omega Challenge

An Alpha's Grace

Follow Sharilyn on Facebook, Instagram, Twitter, Goodreads, and her plain old website.

www.sharilynskye.com

www.ingramcontent.com/pod-product-compliance
Lightning Source LLC
Chambersburg PA
CBHW052029240626
47153CB00006B/2019